What Others Are Saying About
This Doesn't Happen in the Movies by Renée Pawlish

Readers' Favorite Finalist

This is one witty, hilarious detective story that will keep the reader glued to the pages until the very end.

Kirkus Reviews

The promising kickoff to Pawlish's comic mystery series, starring far-from-perfect PI Reed Ferguson. Pawlish earns high marks for plot construction, with twists and turns naturally unfolding as Ferguson, inexperienced but not incapable, feels his way through the case. A good-humored mystery series worth following.

What Others Are Saying About
Nephilim Genesis of Evil by Renée Pawlish

5 Star Review

Stephen King and Dean Koontz have long been known as masters of horror. I believe you can add Renée Pawlish to that list... The plot is entrancing. It grabbed my attention from the beginning and held it to the end.

Readers' Favorite

A Spooky Blend of Biblical Intrigue and Modern Paranormal

This book is clearly written by a pro. The scenes are colored with rich description, depth of character and a cast that is reminiscent of Henry Fonda's *On Golden Pond*. However, there is an evil in this story that FINALLY brings the Nephilim to life and uncovers the dark secrets that Scripture has kept hidden for millennium. If you enjoy reading supernatural fiction that meshes our distant past and the present, you will enjoy this most excellent book.

Kindle Book Review

Nightmare Sally

A Reed Ferguson Mystery

Renée Pawlish

Copyright 2017 by Renée Pawlish
Cover Design copyright by Renée Pawlish

This book is a work of fiction. Names, characters, places, and incidents are either products of the author's imagination or used fictitiously. Any resemblance to actual events, locales, or persons, living or dead, is entirely coincidental. All rights reserved. No part of this publication can be reproduced or transmitted in any form or by any means, electronic or mechanical, without permission in writing from Renée Pawlish.

January 2017

0 9 8 7 6 5 4 3 2 1

ACKNOWLEDGEMENTS

The author gratefully acknowledges all those who helped in the writing of this book, especially: Beth Treat, Janice Horne, Maureen Anderson for technical details in chapter seven, Danny Lynch for serving as the cover model, and Rick Crabtree, for allowing the use of his name. Any mistakes are mine. If I've forgotten anyone, please accept my apologies.

To all my beta readers: I am in your debt!

Maureen Anderson, Bill Baker, Greg Ballinger, Suzanne S. Barnhill, Van Brollini, Jean Brown, Jan Carrico, Rick Crabtree, Irene David, Gwyn Dekker, Kate Dionne, Betty Jo English, Lisa Gall, Tracy Gestewitz, Suzie Glover, Chris Godwin, Patti Gross, Barbara Hackel, Gloria Healey, Kay, Joyce Kahaly, David King, Ray Kline, Cindi Knowles, Maxine Lauer, Lyric McKnight, Debbie McNally, Becky Neilsen, Ann Owen, Janice Paysinger, Charlene Pruett, Fritzi Redgrave, David Richard, Chance Rideout, Mary Lou Romashko, Becky Serna, Tracie Ann Setliff, Andrea Shoemaker, Bev Smith, Al Stevens, Latonya Stewart, Joyce Stumpff, Morris Sweet, Patricia Thursby, Georgi Tileston, Jo Trowbridge, Shelly Voss, Sharon Williams, Lu Wilmot, Mike Wynn, Debbie Young

Nightmare Sally

CHAPTER ONE

She looked nervous.

That was my first impression as I watched her for a moment from the entryway of the Cherry Hills Country Club restaurant.

"May I help you, sir?" a hostess in dark slacks and a white blouse asked me.

"I'm meeting someone," I said, then gestured at the woman, who was sitting near a window across the room.

"Ah, yes. Are you Reed Ferguson?"

I nodded.

"Mrs. Evans is expecting you."

She escorted me to Mrs. Evans's table, then said to her, "Your guest has arrived."

Mrs. Evans thanked the hostess, then indicated I should sit down.

I introduced myself and she smiled.

"Call me Brenda."

She discreetly sized me up, probably wondering how could this brown-haired guy with boring hazel eyes be a private investigator.

If my guess was correct, Brenda Evans was in her fifties. That was maybe ten years or so younger than my mother, but you wouldn't have known it by looking at her. Her cream-colored pantsuit hung loosely on her thin frame, her cheeks were hollow, and her short blond hair had a strange quality I couldn't put my finger on.

"I've met you before, but it was a long time ago," she said.

"I'm sorry, I don't remember."

"When your parents lived in Denver, we golfed here at the club with them."

I nodded, letting her ease into the conversation. A waiter came over and asked if I wanted something to drink. Brenda was sipping coffee, but that wasn't generally my style, and I asked for a Coke. He nodded and scurried away. It was after one on a beautiful September day, and the restaurant was quiet, only a few other diners in the room. The murmur of their conversations drifted into the background as Brenda and I talked.

"I talked to your mother the other day on the phone and was telling her about my ... situation," she said, "and she suggested I contact you."

I leaned in a bit. "I'm happy to help if I can."

"Your mother speaks very highly of you. She says you're quite the detective."

"That's nice to hear."

And it was. My parents had been slow to warm up to the idea of my being a private investigator, but now that I had been in the business for several years, they were coming around. Brenda interrupted my thoughts.

"But she does say that she worries about your getting into dangerous situations."

There it is, I thought. That was the one thing with my mother that wouldn't go away. She always assumed that when I was working on a case, somehow I would end up getting hurt. I'm sure she was sitting on the balcony of her Florida condo right now, wondering what kind of precarious situation I was in.

Brenda smiled. "I assure you, there's nothing dangerous in what I'm asking you to do."

"Okay," I said. "What do you need?"

"I want you to get a message to my daughter."

I watched her twist a gold ring on a bony finger. The waiter returned with my Coke and asked if I wanted anything to eat. Brenda wasn't eating, so I declined.

"We – my husband, Joel, and I," she continued after the waiter left, "haven't had contact with her in months. She barely talks to us." Sadness spread across her pale face.

"What's her name?"

"Sally. I don't think you ever met her."

I couldn't recall if I had. "Tell me about her." I drank some Coke and waited.

She gazed past me, a faraway look in tired brown eyes. "She was a good kid, overall, didn't cause us a lot of trouble. Not like her older brother, Wayne – he was a holy terror. Thank goodness he got things straightened out. He's a lawyer now, lives in San Francisco."

I prodded her back to the original subject. "But Sally?"

"She graduated high school and went to college for a couple of years at Princeton – that's where Joel and Wayne went – but she dropped out and came back to Denver. She wanted to pursue a singing career." She frowned. "So that's what she did. We let her take a year off, thinking it was just a passing fancy, that she'd realize how tough it is to break into that kind of career. We also thought she'd realize…" She glanced away.

"What?"

She couldn't look me in the eye. "Sally's not a very good singer. I hate to say that, but she doesn't have what it takes. She doesn't have the right kind of voice. But she thought she did, and she wouldn't think of going back to college. That led to problems."

"What happened?"

Now she met my gaze. "One night we had an argument about it. Joel and I told her that we didn't think she had the talent to make it in the music industry, and that she needed to think about a real career. And we said in no uncertain terms that if she was going to live under our roof, and have us help pay for her expenses, she needed to drop the singing nonsense and go back to school. Otherwise, she would need to pay rent or move out." She stopped.

I cocked an eyebrow. "She chose to move out."

Her lips trembled, and she took a tissue from a small purse on the table and dabbed at her eyes. Then she clutched it in her hand. "Yes. Joel and I were so certain she wouldn't want to strike out on her own at twenty, and that she'd decide to go back to school. But she didn't. A week later, when Joel was at work, I came home and she'd moved all her belongings out while I was gone. We called her friends, and their parents, and we finally found out she'd rented a tiny attic apartment on Capitol Hill. We went to talk to her, and she said that she'd made her choice, and she wasn't going to take a penny from us, that she was going to live her own life. And to her credit, she has, although I think it's been a struggle for her."

"How long ago was this?"

"Eight years."

"Any issues with drugs or alcohol?"

She shrugged. "She's never said anything, but I think so. I'm not naïve."

"And the singing career?"

She sipped some coffee, then put her cup down. "It never really went anywhere. We didn't talk to her much." She shrugged. "She didn't want to see us; she was angry at us. She worked in some clubs around town, and we heard that she went out to LA for a year or so, and that things might've been going somewhere. But I think things fell apart out there, so she came back to Denver. I don't even know if she plays in clubs anymore. From what I've heard, her old friends don't talk to her now. She periodically calls Wayne, and the last she told him, she was mostly waiting tables."

"Where?"

"I don't know."

"What does Wayne think about the ... situation?"

She sighed. "When she moved out, he thought we were too hard on her. Now he thinks she needs to let go of her anger toward us. He told her that, and that didn't make her happy. None of us have seen or heard from her in over six months, and even when we did, we didn't really talk about anything. She's so angry with Joel and me, but I want her to know that he and I are sorry for what we said and did. We should've been behind her dreams, instead of being critical of her." She drew in a burdened breath, then choked out, "I want her to know that now. It's time to put everything behind us, before it's too late."

She scratched carefully at a spot on her head, and the action seemed to move an entire portion of her hair. Then it dawned on me that she was wearing a wig. Things fell into place.

"I hope this isn't too forward of me," I said gently, "but may I ask, are you having some health issues, and is this why you want to talk to your daughter as soon as you can?"

Her face remained impassive, and then she nodded slowly.

"I have cancer," she finally whispered. "It doesn't look good."

"I'm sorry," I murmured.

She composed herself and shrugged. "It is what it is. I'm a fighter, so we'll see. But I don't want to leave things this way with Sally. That's a burden I can't bear."

"Why do you want me to tell her all this instead of you?"

"I *don't*, but she won't talk to me. I've tried calling her, but her cell phone's disconnected, and I can't find a listing for a new one. I'm sure she has a new number, but I don't know what it is. Both Joel and I have been over to her apartment on separate occasions and she doesn't answer. When I was there, I wondered if she was home because I thought I heard her behind the door. I think she knew it was me and wouldn't answer." She pointed at me. "But you could go over. Since she doesn't know you, she'll probably answer the door, and you can tell her what I've told you."

I thought for a moment. "What exactly would you want me to say to her?"

"You've got to impress upon her that her father and I are sorry, and we're desperate to talk to her. You can let her know I'm having some health issues, if that would help, but don't tell her how serious my condition is. I'd rather do that myself."

I'd rather you do it, too, I thought but didn't say.

"I'm happy to pay you for your time."

I shook my head. "That's not necessary. I don't mind helping out."

"Your mother said you'd say that. It's very kind of you." She dabbed at her eyes with the tissue again. "I just want to clear things up with Sally before it's too late."

"I understand."

She pushed a piece of paper across the table. "This is my contact information, and her address and the only phone number I have for her."

I glanced at it. Brenda lived in Castle Pines, a very nice area south of Denver, and Sally lived in an apartment northeast of downtown, near Bruce Randolph Avenue and York Street. Not the best part of town.

"Does she still live there?"

She arched her eyebrows, surprised. "I think so. I suppose it's possible she moved, but if so, she didn't tell anyone."

"Just checking. One other thing. What does Sally look like?"

She let out a small laugh. "Oh, that would be helpful, huh." She pulled out her phone, swiped at the screen, then handed it to me. "This was taken about a year ago at our house."

Sally Evans was sitting at a picnic table, holding a beer and smiling mischievously. She had shoulder-length brown hair, brown eyes that sparkled the way I'm sure her mother's once did, and the same high cheekbones.

"Wayne was there as well, and she was telling some jokes." She smiled. "She can make you laugh, and Wayne could get her going."

"I can see the resemblance between you two," I said.

She nodded. "Please let me know as soon as you talk to her."

"I will." I folded the paper and put it in my pocket. "Can I pay you for my drink?" I didn't think she'd let me, but I had to ask.

"Don't be silly."

I stood up. "Thank you."

"It's the least I can do."

"I'll be in touch soon."

She smiled wanly, and I walked toward the entryway, then glanced back.

Brenda was staring out the window, the same sad expression on her face.

CHAPTER TWO

This should be easy, I thought as I walked out to my car.

I had just wrapped up a case where I'd helped a coworker of my wife Willie – real name Willimena – find her mother, whom she'd never met. I'd never admit this to my mother, but that case had had a bit of danger involved, and in truth, I was looking for something rather mundane to do now. Helping Brenda Evans seemed to fill the bill.

I got in my 4-Runner and headed north on University Boulevard, and while I drove, I called a familiar number.

"Well, Reed, dear, isn't this a surprise," my mother said in her high-pitched voice. I could tell by her tone that she wasn't surprised that I'd called. After all, she'd known I was going to meet with her friend, and she'd assumed I'd be calling her about it. "You met with Mrs. Evans?"

"I just did," I said.

"How is she? She didn't sound very well on the phone. Did she tell you about her ... condition?"

"She has cancer."

"Yes. It's so sad. I think she's putting on a brave face, but it doesn't look good. And so young, too. I just can't believe it. How did she look? Oh, I hate to think." When my mother gets going, she sometimes forgets to breathe.

"She's pretty frail right now."

"Oh, cancer is such an *awful* thing! Just terrible! It has to be *so* hard on her. And when she brought up this situation with Sally, I thought you might be able to help her so she won't worry. The worrying can't be good for her health."

"I understand. I'm headed to Sally's apartment now to deliver a message from Brenda."

"That's nice, dear. I knew I could count on you."

I moved into private-eye mode. "How well do you know the Evans?"

"Mostly socializing at the club, and we talk on the phone sometimes. Why do you ask?"

"Just trying to get a feel for Sally before I meet her face to face. I'd like to know what she's like."

"Hmm, let me think. I remember seeing her a time or two at the club, with Brenda. She was maybe eighteen at the time. She was quite the stinker, if you ask me – a bit spoiled – but please don't tell Brenda I said that."

"Your secret's safe with me."

"Thank you, dear. Anyway, Sally was a bit standoffish, but very pretty. I thought at one time – if she'd been a bit older – the two of you might've made a nice couple. But then Brenda would hint at how they were having some problems with Sally, and I was glad dating you wasn't an option. And then we'd never have met Willie. She's so sweet."

"Yes, she is," I concurred, knowing that there wasn't any woman but Willie for me. "Did Brenda ever talk about Sally's singing career?"

"Just in general terms, that it was Sally's dream, but they didn't think she had the talent to go anywhere with it, that sort of thing."

"Did they talk about Sally doing drugs or alcohol?"

"Hmm, I don't recall that. But Brenda did say Sally had been dating a guy they weren't too fond of."

"When was this?"

"About six months ago. That was the last time they saw Sally. The boyfriend was there, and he didn't impress Brenda. She said he was aloof, and a bit mean to Sally. She couldn't see what Sally saw in the guy."

"Brenda didn't mention that."

"I assume she was embarrassed by it."

"That's probably it," I said, even though, as the ace detective, it made me suspicious. Never assume anything.

"What was the boyfriend's name?"

"I don't recall her mentioning that."

I moved on. "What's your impression of Joel Evans?"

"He's a lawyer, but I don't know much beyond that. When I saw him at the club, he was maybe a bit cold at times. I mostly socialized with Brenda. Why?"

"Just curious." I thought for a moment. "Well, hopefully Sally is around, and she'll give me a few minutes of her time."

"I hope so. You'll let Brenda know the minute you find out anything, right?"

"Yes, Mother."

"I knew Brenda could count on you. And for once, it doesn't sound dangerous."

"No, Mother, it doesn't."

I chatted with her for a few minutes longer, then talked to my father for a bit. He caught me up on his golf game, and the weather. Then I heard my mother calling him, and I ended the call. I turned on the stereo and listened to The Smiths, my favorite '80s alternative band, while I continued north. It was a straight shot up University, which turned into Josephine, and then York. I finally turned on Bruce Randolph and went east.

The address Brenda Evans had provided me was a two-building apartment complex on Columbine Street. Each building was three stories, built with a haphazard mix of tan and brown brick. The rest of the neighborhood consisted of tiny houses that were better kept than the apartment complex. I was struck by the lack of trees, shrubs, or any other foliage in the complex. It gave the buildings a stark, isolated feel.

I parked down the block, and the late summer sun was hot as I crossed the street. Farther up the block, some kids were walking home from school, but otherwise it was quiet. I went up a walkway between the buildings. Two of the downstairs units had doors that opened into the common area. Sally lived in the north building in unit 102, toward the back. I walked up a short sidewalk to her door and knocked. No one answered. A scrawny black kitten dashed up near me and then ran off. I smiled, then knocked on the door again. Still no answer. I stepped back and gave the building a once-over. I didn't see anyone looking out any windows, and no one was in the common area, so I moved over to a window next to the door and peeked in.

Cheap curtains were open, and I could see what appeared to be an old couch against a wall, and a TV across from it, sitting on a cheap stand. At the back was a kitchen. But no people. I went back to the door and knocked, not expecting any answer. When none came, I went to the center of the north building where there was a door that led into a small foyer.

It wasn't as quiet in here. Down a hallway, rock music blared from behind a door. Up a set of stairs, a woman yelled and a door slammed shut. I glanced around, and found a bank of mailboxes. I checked them, but they weren't labeled except for the manager's, who lived in 103. Then a loud voice from upstairs said, "I don't need you. I'll take all of it and you got nothing."

Heavy footsteps sounded on the stairs, and a young guy in torn jeans, a black T-shirt, and tattoos on his arms appeared. He muttered, "I got the material. I'll do it myself." He scowled as he lit a cigarette.

"Excuse me?" I said.

He almost didn't stop, but started to push through the door. He glared at me, then tossed his head so that his long bangs were out of his eyes. "Yeah?"

"Does Sally Evans still lives in 102?"

He eyed me suspiciously. "Who?"

"Sally Evans. She's about five-five, long brown hair."

He shrugged. "I don't know, man."

He swore at me and went out the door.

"So much for that," I muttered.

Before the door shut, the black kitten dashed in.

"You lost, buddy?" I asked him. Or maybe it was a her. I wasn't sure.

It meowed at me and walked around between my legs.

"Hey, come here." I reached down to pick it up, but it dashed up the stairs and disappeared.

I shrugged, walked down the hall, and checked 103 – the manager's apartment – without success, then went to 104 and banged on the door where the rock music was coming from. The music stayed at its intense volume, and no one answered. I knocked a few more times before giving up. I stood for a moment, wondering why the manager didn't do anything about the music. Then I went to the second floor and started rapping on doors. I had success at the second apartment. The door flew open to reveal a short woman with kinky blond hair and dark eye shadow.

"Gary, I told you to beat it or I'll – oh." She stared at me with her mouth open, then glanced to another stairwell opposite the one I'd used. "Waddaya want?"

"I'm hoping you might be able to help me," I said. "Do you know if Sally Evans still live in 102?"

"Is that the woman downstairs on the end? That Sally?"

I nodded.

"I haven't seen her around in a while."

"How long?"

She shrugged. "I don't know. A month or so."

"She moved out?"

"I don't think so, I just haven't seen her."

"Do you know where she works?"

She gnawed at her lip. "She was waiting tables at the Rat, but I haven't seen her in there in a while, either."

"The Rat?"

"The Rat Tavern, near Forty-second and Steele."

"Was she still singing?"

"Singing?" She was completely puzzled by the question.

"She used to sing at some clubs."

"That's news to me. Listen, I gotta go."

"Okay, thanks," I said, but the door had already slammed in my face.

I trudged back downstairs. As I opened the foyer door, the kitten appeared out of nowhere and slipped outside. I followed him and looked around. The man I'd seen in the foyer was long gone, and the common area was still empty. I walked back to my car, got in, then pulled out my cell phone. I spent a few minutes trying to find a phone number for Sally Evans. All I could find was the number I had, which wasn't active. I finally gave up, dialed a familiar number, and waited.

"What's up, O Great Detective?"

This is how my best friend, Cal Whitmore, typically greet me. I'd tried to talk him into other nicknames, but nothing else stuck.

"How're you doing?" I asked.

"Good. I'm working for a company now to see if I can break into their systems. They think they've got everything locked down good, but I've already found a way in." There was a satisfied tone in his voice.

Cal and I have been friends since we were kids, and he is practically family – my mother treats him like another son. He's a recluse, preferring to stay in his house in the mountains west of Denver. He owns his own consulting firm and specializes in computer security, and he can get into almost any system, even government ones. He's a hacker, but he hates being called that. Because of his skill sets, I sometimes ask for his help to find information that would take me too much time to figure out, or that I couldn't access at all. And the truth is, he likes to assist, although he would never admit it.

"Do you have time for a favor?" I asked.

"Sure thing."

I told him about my meeting with Brenda Evans.

"I don't remember you ever talking about her, or Sally," he said when I finished. It wouldn't have surprised me if he'd met Sally.

"She's about ten years younger than we are."

"Oh," he said. "That explains it. We wouldn't have hung around with her back then."

"You wouldn't have been interested in her if we had," I said. "You never notice any woman."

"True."

"Can you see if you can find her phone number for me?" I asked. "If I could get that, then I don't have to search for her."

"Sally Evans? Evans is a pretty common name." I heard him typing in the background. "Hmm. There's a Sally Evans who's an artist, but she lives in Florida. Let's see, here's a few others. None in Denver, though. Where does she live?"

I gave him the address.

"Give me a while and I'll see what I can find."

"I'll call you later."

"That'll work." And he was gone.

I sat for a minute, wondering about my next move. I could leave things as they were. After all, I'd tried to make contact with Sally, with no luck. But the reality was I could put in at least a little more effort to help out Brenda Evans. It seemed the least I could do.

So, what were my options? I could sit in the 4-Runner and wait for a while to see if Sally came home. I could also wait to see if Cal was able to find her number. Then something occurred to me. The upstairs neighbor had said Sally was working at the Rat Tavern. Maybe she was there now. If so, I could talk to her, deliver Brenda's message, and then be finished with this little case.

I looked up the address for the Rat Tavern, started the 4-Runner, and drove off.

CHAPTER THREE

It didn't take me long to arrive at the Rat Tavern, as it was only a mile or so north of Sally's apartment. As I drove up Steele Street, I was struck by how the neighborhood was changing. At one time, this had been a mostly industrial and lower income part of town, with tiny, rundown houses flanked by warehouses to the north. Now, although some homes were still in need of attention, many more were better attended to, and several houses were being razed to make way for new ones.

When I reached Forty-second Street, I glanced around. I didn't see the Rat Tavern, so I drove east. On the left side of the street were small, single-story warehouses and industrial buildings, and across the street were small houses.

Not the view I'd want from my front yard, I thought.

I'd apparently turned the wrong way, so I turned around and headed west. Four blocks from Steele, I spotted the Rat Tavern. The bar was definitely a hole-in-the-wall, nothing more than a tiny, oddly shaped cinderblock building. On the corner, a pay phone still sat outside. I wondered if the phone actually worked. Above the door, black letters said "Tavern."

It was almost four o'clock, and there were no spaces in front of the bar. I parked next door in front of an auto supply warehouse, got out and made sure to lock the 4-Runner, then walked back to the bar. As I neared the entrance, two young guys in baggy shorts and T-shirts walked out of the bar and stood on the corner, smoking cigarettes. They stared at me as I passed them and went inside.

The Rat Tavern consisted of nothing more than a few round tables, a bar against the wall opposite the door, and two booths by windows that faced the street. A waitress in a tight T-shirt and some very short jean shorts was bustling between tables. The crowd was younger, mostly African-American and Hispanic, their attire mostly T-shirts and shorts or tight jeans, their voices loud over a pounding bass beat that sounded from overhead speakers. I immediately felt glances that took in my tan slacks, white shirt, and black shoes.

I let my eyes adjust to the dim light, then moseyed up to the bar. I waited while a bartender – a tall woman with mocha skin and spindly arms – served drinks for two Hispanic women who made no bones about sizing me up as the stranger I was. I gave them a friendly nod, then signaled the bartender.

"What'll it be?" she said loudly over the music. She was older, with crow's feet at the corners of her eyes and hair graying at the roots, but her voice was low and sultry.

I ordered my usual microbrew. "Fat Tire."

An eyebrow arched. "Don't got that."

"A Budweiser," I amended my order.

She gave me the faintest of derisive smiles, then reached under the bar and extracted a longneck bottle. She deftly popped the lid off and put it down in front of me.

"Two bucks."

I paid her, took a sip of the beer, then put it down. She took the money and stuffed it in a register, and as she did so, she kept her eyes on me.

"I'm looking for someone," I said, speaking up over the din.

She put sinewy hands with long fingernails on the bar. "I didn't think you happened in here just for a drink."

"I'm that obvious?" I joked.

She snorted, then shook her head. "I'm not getting anyone in trouble, if you know what I mean."

I held up a hand. "No trouble. There's a woman who works here named Sally Evans."

"Nightmare Sally?" There was disappointment in the tone.

That gave me pause. I couldn't help but think about a film noir called *Nightmare Alley*. It starred Tyrone Power as con man Stanton Carlisle and Joan Blondell as carny Mademoiselle Zeena. Carlisle and Zeena create a mentalist act and they scam people out of money, but all the lying and deception tear Carlisle apart, and he ends up a drunk at the end of the movie.

"Nightmare Sally?" I finally repeated. "Why do you call her that?"

She snickered. "I shouldn't have, but even she agreed that she was a nightmare and laughed about it. That's how everyone around here referred to her, because she was just that – a nightmare. Talk about a flake. And she don't work here anymore."

"What happened?" I said.

"I fired her."

"Why?"

"It didn't work out."

"How long did she work here?"

"Maybe a year. Almost a year too long."

I took another sip of my beer. "You manage the place?"

"I own it, for twenty years. It isn't much, just a place for the neighborhood to come in and take a load off, grab some food, get drunk at night before they go home, and I manage to pay my bills from it. And I don't got any more time for someone like Sally."

She said it as if she thought it would end the conversation. But I didn't give up that easily.

"What was the problem with her?" I went on.

She leaned in and stared at me. "Why're you looking for her?"

I hesitated. "Her mother's been trying to find her. They're sort of estranged, but her mother has some news she'd like to tell Sally."

She tipped her head as she studied me, and a dawning flashed in her eyes. "Something wrong with her mother?"

She was perceptive.

"Yeah, something like that."

She gave me a long, pensive gaze, then glanced past me and hollered at the waitress. "Annie?" The waitress came over. "Watch things for me."

"Sure thing, Ella," Annie said.

Annie nodded and came around the end of the bar. Ella poured herself a soda, then gestured for me to follow her. She opened a door at the end of the bar and looked at me. I left my beer on the bar and followed her through a kitchen where a rotund guy in a greasy apron was frying burgers on a large stove. Ella crossed the kitchen and went through another door, and we stepped out into a small lot behind the building.

She shut the door and took a few steps away from it, then turned and looked at me. "If I'm going to talk to you, I'm not going to shout."

I nodded, appreciating the sudden silence.

She gave me a thoughtful look. "You a detective?"

"Private investigator."

"I see."

"You don't have a problem telling me about Sally?"

She shrugged, then sipped her soda. "I feel sorry for her."

"Why?"

She waved a hand to encompass the bar and surroundings. "Look around. This isn't a place for someone like Sally. That girl had her some education, a good upbringing. But she hit on hard times, and I knew she could use the money ..." She shrugged. "I hired her."

"But you regretted it."

"I didn't mind giving her a chance – hell, someone gave me a chance when I needed it. But she was too much. She wouldn't come in on time, or sometimes at all. She messed up orders, and that's saying something, since we don't serve too many beers, and the menu don't got but a few things on it. She like to drove me nuts. I gave her so many chances, but I finally had to let her go."

I took a second to gather my thoughts. "How'd you meet Sally? Did she come in here looking for work?"

She shook her head. "Nah. She showed up now and again with Gabe – that's the guy she was dating."

"You don't like Gabe?"

"No."

"Why not?"

"For one, he's immature, and too young for her. He tries to be a charmer, but I don't buy it. He's a high-school dropout, goes from job to job, and girlfriend to girlfriend. Every time you turn around, he's bragging about the next big thing that's gonna make him rich."

"Like what?"

"Mostly it's that he's gonna produce a music CD and be a star. That's his big thing. Music. It never pans out, but he always has money."

"Did you know Sally wanted to be a singer?"

She sipped some soda. "Yep. That was one of the things she said about Gabe, that he had talent and between the two of them, they were going to make it big. I got the feeling she hadn't sung in any clubs in a while, not that she'd have to. With the internet, you can put up videos and songs, and get discovered that way. She had me watch a video Gabe helped her produce, but it wasn't much good." She laughed and pointed at the bar. "Although what passes for music these days is different than in my time, so what do I know? I'd just as soon be playing Etta James, or Ella Fitzgerald – that's who I was named after – than that crap that's on now. But the kids like it."

"I hear you," I said, suddenly feeling old. I couldn't identify half the songs on the radio these days. I preferred hanging out at B 52's, a pool hall near my condo that favored '80s music. I sighed at how out-of-place I felt at the Rat, then resumed my questions. "Is Gabe dealing drugs, or doing something else illegal that would make money for him?"

She shrugged. She was willing to talk, but she wasn't going to tell me everything.

"What's his last name?"

"I don't know."

"What's Sally like?" I asked. "Besides the nightmare part."

She sighed. "She actually seems like a good kid, underneath, but she don't make good choices. Like Gabe. They're not right for each other, not at all, but you couldn't tell her that."

"She probably hooked up with him because of the music."

"Yeah, but..." Sadness flickered in her eyes. "I think he hit her some. I'd see her in here, trying to cover up bruises with makeup. But then, she might've held her own because Gabe had a black eye one time, and a scratch on his face another." She twisted up her lips. "That Gabe. You got to put a whole lotta gone between you and someone like that."

"Did Sally do drugs?"

She glanced away. "Maybe some pot, but not anything harder, at least not that I ever heard her say. That wasn't the problem. She just wasn't reliable and she had no direction, no gumption. You got a dream, you got to work hard to make it reality. It don't just happen." A faraway look leaped into her eyes. "Trust me, I know that."

I nodded. "When's the last time you saw her?"

"Oh, maybe a month ago. That's when I told her not to bother coming in anymore. She took off and hasn't been back."

"What about Gabe?"

"He comes in now and again, but he knows I see through his BS, so he doesn't tell me anything."

"What's he look like?"

"He's not very tall, and he's got longer hair that falls into his eyes. And tattoos on his arms."

"That sounds like a guy I saw at Sally's apartment. Too bad I hadn't known it was him, or I could've asked him for Sally's phone number."

"Right." She gulped down the last of her soda, then gestured at the back door. "I got to get back in there."

"If Sally's going to mend fences with her mother, she better do it soon," I said.

She nodded slowly. "If I see her, I'll tell her that."

"Do you have her phone number?"

She pulled out a cell phone, scrolled through it, then rattled off a number. It was the inactive number that Brenda had.

"That's not her current number."

"Oh."

"She's living over on Columbine Street, right?"

She shrugged. "That I don't know."

"Thanks," I said. I handed her a business card and asked her to call me if she heard from Sally.

She stared at the card for a second, then tucked it into her bra.

"You coming back inside?"

I shook my head. She gave me a wan smile, downed her soda and went back into the bar. After she left, I walked around the side of the building and back to my car.

CHAPTER FOUR

Nightmare Sally, I thought as I drove away from the Rat Tavern. She sounded like quite the person. I wondered if Brenda knew what people thought of her daughter. Something occurred to me. Had Sally been more of a flake growing up than Brenda had let on? Had Brenda left that part out when she'd talked about Sally?

I shrugged. It didn't really matter. That part wasn't my business, and knowing it or not didn't prevent me from delivering a message to Sally. A message that was turning out to be harder to deliver than I'd expected.

I decided to go back to Sally's apartment building and give one last shot at finding her. If she didn't show up, I'd call it a night. I headed down Columbine Street and soon came to her place. I parked in front, walked around to her unit, and knocked on her door again. Still no answer, so I went back to the 4-Runner, played a mix of '80s favorites, and waited.

The street grew busier, and so did the courtyard between the buildings. Two men in jeans emerged from the south building and sat in front of their unit in lawn chairs drinking beer. A few kids played catch with a football nearby, and the men watched them play. The neighborhood may have been a little rough, but it seemed that people kept an eye out for each other. At 5:30, a woman in gray slacks and a sleeveless blouse sauntered into the courtyard. She waved at the men and started up the walk to 102. I hurried out of the car, ducked around the kids, and ran toward her.

"Excuse me?" I said.

She was just opening her door and she whirled around and stared at me. She squinted at me distrustfully. "Yes?"

I gestured at her door. "You live there?"

"Who wants to know?"

I sensed movement behind me, and I turned partway around. One of the two beer-drinking guys had quietly crossed the courtyard and was staring at me, a can of Coors still in his hand.

"Problem?" he said to the woman.

She crossed her arms and glared at me. "Is there?"

I shook my head slowly. "I'm looking for Sally Evans." I pointed behind her. "I was told she lives there."

"Who?" She appeared genuinely puzzled. "I just moved in." The black kitten I'd seen earlier walked into the courtyard and up to us. The woman shooed at it. "That little stray's been hanging around for days. Don't know where it came from." It darted back.

"Sally ain't here anymore," the man said. "She's been gone a few weeks."

"Where'd she move to?"

He shrugged. "How the hell should I know? She didn't tell me anything. Maybe the manager knows."

"I gotta go," the woman said.

She stepped inside her apartment and the door slammed shut. The man continued to stare at me.

"It's important I get a message to Sally," I said. "It's about a family matter."

"Good luck with that." He took a sip of beer, crushed the can in his hand, and tossed the can toward the kitten, who dashed away. "She's gone."

I glared at him, not happy at him trying to hit the kitten with his beer can. "You knew her?"

"I guess."

"What was she like?"

He'd already headed back to his chair. "She's a flake."

"Do you know Gabe? Her boyfriend?"

He stopped and glanced over his shoulder. "I don't know what she was doin' with him."

"Why is that?"

"Man, this ain't Dr. Phil. Get lost."

His friend guffawed as he sat down. They made a point of not looking at me as I walked away. They were laughing by the time I went inside the north building. The loud rock music I'd heard earlier had been replaced by sounds from a television. I walked down the hall to the manager's door, and the TV noise grew louder. I banged on the door and waited. A moment later, it opened to reveal a stout man with salt-and-pepper hair and thick glasses. A TV blared in Spanish in the background.

"Yes?" He had the trace of an accent.

"You're the manager?" I asked.

"Yes. There are no apartments available."

I shook my head. "I'm trying to find Sally Evans. She lived in 102."

He ran a thumb and index finger around the edges of his mouth, then held a hand to his ear. I started to talk again and he stopped me, then spun around and disappeared down a short hall. The sound of the TV stopped, and he reappeared.

"What's that?"

"Sally Evans," I said.

"Sure, I know her. She moved out."

"When?"

"About a month ago."

That was close to what the man in the courtyard had said. "Did she leave a forwarding address?"

"A what?" He cupped a hand to his ear again.

No wonder the TV was loud.

I raised my voice. "Did she tell you her new address?"

"Oh." He shook his head. "I don't know where she went."

"Do you have a phone number for her?"

"Hmm." He did the thumb and finger thing again. "Who are you?"

He was being careful now. I pulled out my wallet and flashed my private investigator's license at him. His Adam's apple bobbed as he gulped, and he stood a little straighter.

"I need to get in touch with Sally," I said. "It's important."

"Yes, I see. Let me get that number for you."

He scurried away, and I heard drawers opening. He came back with a file, and he opened it, then ran his finger along a page. "This is the number."

As he read it off the page, I immediately knew it was the wrong one. He probably never bothered to update his tenant information.

"Does that help?" he asked.

"It's no longer in service," I said.

"Oh." He gave me a blank look.

"Was Sally a good tenant?"

"She was okay, but she got behind on her rent once in a while, and I'd have to threaten to evict her." He frowned. "I hate doing that. I'm only doing this to supplement my social security, and I don't want any problems with anyone. I let them be, and I don't get involved in anything if I don't have to. But when someone gets behind on the rent, or they get the cops here, it makes it hard for me."

"Did someone call the cops on Sally?"

"Her, and some others. It happens."

"What was Sally doing that someone called on her?"

He sighed. "A problem with her boyfriend."

"Gabe?" I described him.

"Yeah, that's the one." A tinge of fear entered his voice. "He was here off and on."

"You were scared of him?"

His lips formed a tight line, and he nodded. "One time, I told them they were making too much noise, and he had a gun. He threatened me." He glanced away. "You see why I don't want to make hassles with the people around here? I just want to keep a roof over my head, you know?"

I nodded sympathetically, in part because I wanted to keep him talking, but I also felt genuinely sorry for him.

"Have you seen Gabe since she moved out?"

"I don't remember the last time I saw him."

"You said Sally got behind on her rent," I went on.

"Yeah, but she always managed to come up with the money before I had to kick her out."

"How'd she come up with it?"

He shrugged. "She didn't tell me, and I didn't ask."

"Did you have any other problems with her?"

"Well … she could play her music pretty loud, but never as bad as that guy." He pointed toward the door to 104. "He can play it loud, but it's during the day, and most people are gone to work. And I don't hear it."

I'll bet, I thought. "I understand Sally was an aspiring musician."

"A what?"

I raised my voice. "She wanted to be a singer."

"Oh, yeah. She liked to sit out in the courtyard and play her guitar and sing. I don't think anyone really thought much of it. I know Gabe didn't."

"Why do you say that?"

He scowled. "The look on his face when he watched her play. He wasn't impressed."

"Did you like her music?"

"I never listened to it."

"Did the two of them fight a lot?"

He nodded. "I think so, but I don't get involved."

"Did they do drugs?"

"I don't know. Probably. If you want to talk to him, he comes around sometimes. He hangs out with the guy in 202."

"Good to know," I said.

Somewhere in the apartment, a phone rang.

He glanced over his shoulder. "I should get that."

"The guy in 202. What's his name?"

"Adam."

"Adam what?"

He took a step back and started to close the door.

"If you see Sally," I said as I quickly pulled a business card from my wallet, "can you ask her to call me?"

"Sure." He took the card and stuffed it into his pants pocket. By the look on his face, I wondered if he would pass along the message or not. As he'd clearly indicated, he did not want to get mixed up in anything. I doubted I'd hear from him.

He dismissed me with a hand, and the door shut.

I stood in the hallway for a moment, thinking. I hadn't been able to deliver Brenda's message to Sally, and it appeared that I wouldn't be able to anytime soon because – as I'd discovered – Sally was gone.

But how much more poking around should I do? Sally didn't live here anymore, and that was that. Would Brenda want me to keep looking? With those thoughts in my mind, I went outside. I felt the eyes of the two beer-drinkers on me as I hurried back to my car.

CHAPTER FIVE

As I got in the 4-Runner, Humphrey Bogart's voice said, "Oh, it's not always easy to know what to do." How apt. My ringtone was a sound clip from Sam Spade in *The Maltese Falcon*. I am a huge Bogie fan, and always wish I could be as cool as he was in all his old film noir movies that I love so much.

I looked at the number. It was Cal.

"What's up, O Great Clandestine Information Specialist?" I said.

He snickered. "The only number I can find for Sally Evans is disconnected because she wasn't paying her bill." That was Cal, no nonsense, get right to the point.

"That's a bummer, but I'm not surprised. What about an address?"

"She's on Columbine Street."

"Not anymore."

"She moved?"

"She seems to have disappeared within the last few weeks. No one knows where she is."

"Until she starts paying bills again with a new address, I won't be able to help you," he said.

"Those are rare words."

He laughed again. "Even *I* can only do so much."

"I appreciate you trying."

"No problem. Let me know if you need anything else." With that, he ended the call.

I sat for a moment longer and called Brenda Evans. She answered with a tentative "hello."

"It's Reed Ferguson," I said as I watched the men in the courtyard. They didn't look happy that I was still there.

"Did you talk to her?" Brenda asked quickly.

"No. I couldn't find her."

"Would you try again another time?"

"She doesn't live at that apartment anymore."

"Where is she?"

"I don't know."

"When did she move out?"

"About three to four weeks ago."

"Was she in trouble?"

I hesitated. I really didn't know, but I didn't want to worry her, either. "I don't think so. She's just gone."

She sighed heavily. "I wonder when she was planning on telling us she moved."

"You might hear from her soon."

"I don't have time to wait. I'll hire you to find her."

I thought she might say that. "I can do some more looking around. It might take a few days."

"So you've already started searching for her?"

"Well, sort of." I filled Brenda in on what I'd done since I'd seen her at the club.

"It sounds like things still aren't going well for Sally," she said when I finished. The ache in her tone was clear.

"Do you know about this man Gabe?" I asked.

"She brought him to the house the last time I saw her. I didn't mention it because I didn't think it mattered. I have no idea how to get in touch with him."

"If I can find him, that'll likely lead me to her," I mused. Brenda didn't say anything to that. I thought more about her daughter. "Was Sally always…" I paused.

"Flaky?"

"Yes."

It took her a moment to answer. "Well, she kind of was as a kid, but I didn't want to paint her in a bad light. I suppose we might've spoiled her some." That fit with what my mother had told me. "Maybe the flakiness has something to do with her artistic side, but she wasn't that easy to deal with."

"I understand."

"I hope that doesn't cause you more problems with finding her."

I chuckled. "Let's hope not."

"Let me know what you find out." She didn't sound hopeful.

"I will."

I ended the call and got back out of the 4-Runner. As I returned to the courtyard, the two men stared at me.

"Man, you looking for trouble? You need to move on," the man who'd talked to me earlier said. He was starting to slur his words.

"I'll be gone soon," I said. I hurried back into the north building. If I wasn't careful, those two were going to cause *me* trouble.

I took the stairs to the second floor and went to unit 202. I knocked and waited. A moment later, the door opened to reveal a thin young man in khaki shorts that hung low on his hips and a muscle shirt that revealed no muscles.

"Yeah?" he said.

"Are you Adam?"

"Who wants to know?"

His evasiveness wasn't fooling me.

"I'm looking for Sally Evans or Gabe," I said. "The manager says you might know where I can find them." That wasn't true, but how would he know?

"Who?"

"Sally. She lived downstairs."

"I don't know her."

"You know Gabe." I stared hard at him. "He was here earlier today."

"Well, he's not here now."

He started to shut the door, but I put my hand out to stop it from closing.

"Stop lying to me," I said.

"Hey," he said as he tried to push the door shut. "Gabe hangs out at the Rat, okay? It's on–"

"I know where it is," I interrupted. "Where else might he be?"

"I dunno."

"What's Gabe's last name?"

"Culpepper," he said.

I put my hand down and the door slammed in my face. I grimaced. No matter how much I tried, I'd never be as tough as Bogie. I went back downstairs and outside, and was relieved to see that the beer-drinkers were gone. But the kitten was back, and I noticed that it followed me all the way back to the 4-Runner. I opened the door, and before I could climb in, the kitten jumped onto the floorboard and onto my seat.

"No, bud," I said to him. "Don't you have a home around here?"

He sat on the seat and meowed at me. He looked like he could use a meal, but I didn't have anything to give him. I sighed as I picked him up and put him on the sidewalk.

"Go on home," I said.

He stared at me, his tail twitching.

"I'm sorry, I've got to go."

I got in the car and muttered to myself about talking to a cat, then drove up the street toward the Rat Tavern. Maybe Gabe would show up there. I felt like I was running in circles. On the way, I called Willie.

"Hey, babe," she said cheerily. "Where are you?"

"I might be a while," I said. I told her about my meeting with Brenda, and the ensuing case.

"Oh, okay," she said when I finished. "Maybe I'll call Darcy and see if she wants to visit some of the animal shelters and go to dinner. I just love cats. I had a cat when I was a kid, and I loved cuddling with him, and listening to him purr. I miss that, and it would be so nice to have one around here."

Darcy Cranston, Willie's best friend, lives across the street in a Victorian house that has been converted into apartments. Willie owns the house as an investment property, and had lived there until she moved in with me.

Willie had been talking about getting a cat, and her best friend, Darcy, had been encouraging her all along the way and even going with her to visit some animal shelters. I, on the other hand, wasn't so sure I wanted one.

"Are you sure you want a cat?" I said, thinking about the scrawny black kitten.

"Hon, they're so cute, and they're easy to take care of. If we get a cat, you won't regret it."

"Uh-huh." I changed the subject. "I'll try not to be too late. Do you work tomorrow?"

"Yes, but not until the afternoon."

Willie is an ER admissions nurse, and she sometimes has irregular hours. Between her shifts and my own haphazard schedule, it was difficult to find time together.

"How about we open a bottle of wine and watch a movie when I get home?" I asked.

"That'd be nice. I won't stay out too late with Darcy then."

"Great."

I ended the call, and was soon parked outside the Rat Tavern again. When I went inside, the tiny place was packed. I sidled up to the corner of the bar and waited until Ella noticed me. She threw me a small smile, grabbed a Budweiser longneck, and came over.

"You're back," she said as she set down the beer. "It's on the house."

"Thanks."

"You look like you could use it."

I nodded and took a long drink.

"No luck finding Sally?" she asked.

I shook my head. "She's apparently moved, and the only lead I now have is that Gabe sometimes comes in here. But you knew that."

She laughed, then glanced around. "But not so far tonight."

I surveyed the bar. "Does anyone else here know Sally?"

"Yeah, but I already asked them if they knew where she was."

I cocked an eyebrow at her.

"I would've called you if anyone did," she said. "But no one knows her that well, or knows where she is."

"Thanks for checking."

She sighed. "Sure thing." Then she sauntered off to make drinks.

I stayed at my place at the end of the bar and visited off and on with Ella, but in the back of my mind, I kept thinking about the little black kitten. Did he have a home to go to? I sighed and checked my watch. Nine o'clock, and Gabe hadn't shown up. I finally put a big tip on the bar for Ella and left, but instead of heading home, I drove back to Sally's old apartment. I parked and walked up to the building. Music and sounds from TV shows came from open windows. I stood for a moment and then called out quietly, "Here kitty, kitty."

Nothing. Maybe the little guy had a home.

I called out again, then shrugged and walked back to the 4-Runner. I opened the door and right then, a tiny black fur ball materialized out of the darkness and walked around my legs.

"There you are," I said.

I reached out and petted him, and he started to purr.

"I must be crazy," I muttered as I reached down and picked him up.

He nestled in the crook of my arm as I got in and drove away. I was home at our condo in Uptown, a neighborhood just east of downtown, fifteen minutes later. When I walked through the door, Willie was sitting on the couch, her laptop on her lap.

She sat up and yawned. "How'd things go?" She was in her favorite pink robe and her white running socks. I'm not sure how she does it, but she makes even a fleece robe look awfully appealing.

"A dead end," I said. "I'll try again tomorrow."

Then she saw the kitten. "Ooooh! Who do you have?"

She set her laptop on the coffee table, leaped up, hurried over, and took the kitten from me. "Aren't you darling?" she said to it. He meowed and she cooed at him and kissed his head repeatedly.

I grinned. "You're making a spectacle of yourself."

"You're just jealous. Who does he belong to?"

"He's a stray."

She went into the kitchen, still talking to the kitten. "Let's get you something to eat."

I followed her and watched as she got out some lunch meat and broke it into tiny pieces.

"Shouldn't you give him milk?" I asked.

She shook her head. "It can give them runny bowels. Get him a bowl of water."

"I didn't know that," I said as I got a bowl, filled it with water, and set it on the floor.

The kitten lapped at the water, and when Willie put a plate of meat on the floor, he devoured it quickly.

"He's so cute!" she said.

"Uh-huh." I had to admit, he sort of was.

When the kitten finished eating, Willie picked him up, went back into the living room, and sat on the couch. I sat down next to her as she let the kitten snuggle up against her. Then she looked at me.

"You look disappointed," she said. "If we can't find an owner for this kitty, don't you think he'd be a nice addition?"

I shook my head. "It's not that. I feel like I just wasted a day. I have no idea where Sally or her boyfriend are, and I'm not sure how to find them."

"You'll figure it out. You always do."

"To tell you the truth, I don't want to think about it right now."

"You really are bummed."

I didn't say anything for a moment. "People call her 'Nightmare Sally.' When I hear that, all I can think about is *Nightmare Alley*." I told her about the movie, then gestured at the TV. "We could watch it."

"Oh, babe, that sounds like a pretty grim movie." She stared into the kitten's eyes. "Doesn't that sound like too much tonight?" she asked it.

"It is, but it's really a film noir gem and –"

"And it won't help you forget about Sally."

"That's true."

She put her hand on my thigh, and I let my hand slip underneath her robe. The kitten swiped at me.

"Hey," I said to him.

Willie put the kitten at the other end of the couch. "He'll fall asleep."

Then she leaned over and kissed me, and although the kitten interrupted us more than once, I didn't think about Nightmare Sally again that night.

» » » » »

The next day was Thursday, and I spent that day, and the next three, searching for Sally and Gabe. I watched the apartment building on Columbine Street, thinking Gabe might show up. I asked people in the neighborhood if they'd seen either of them, and I also asked around to see if anyone was missing a black kitten. I received negative answers to both. I also checked some of the businesses in the area, but no one knew of either Sally or Gabe. Brenda gave me her son Wayne's number and I talked to him, but he hadn't heard from Sally in weeks. I also spent a lot of time at the Rat Tavern, sitting in the corner, visiting with Ella and drinking Budweiser longnecks, but neither Sally nor Gabe showed up. By Sunday night, I had concluded two things. One, if they didn't show up tonight, I was going to give up. And two, if I wasn't careful, I'd turn into the cliché of the alcoholic PI.

It was close to ten p.m. and I was nursing a glass of Coke when Ella came over to me. She locked eyes with me, then gave a little tip of her head, and I knew what she was telling me. I turned around and looked toward the door.

Gabe Culpepper had just walked into the bar.

CHAPTER SIX

Gabe glanced around the room. He was in jeans and a black leather coat that seemed too much given the nice weather, and I thought he looked even younger than when I'd seen him before. He took a seat at one of the tables, then signaled the waitress and ordered. As she walked away, he pulled out his phone and began texting someone.

I grabbed my Coke, ambled over, and sat down across from him. He looked up, and his eyes narrowed. He'd been described as a charmer, and mean, but no one had captured the essence of his eyes. Even in the brief moment when I studied him, I saw a calculating glint in them, as if he was searching for an angle. He may have been young, but he was already dangerous.

"This table's taken," he said. The tone was decidedly not friendly.

I stared at him, letting him know I wouldn't be intimidated. "We need to talk."

"Who the hell are you?"

"Reed," I said. I wasn't going to tell him I was a private investigator and have him clam up.

"Okay, Reed, get lost. I'm waiting for someone."

I ignored that and took a sip of my Coke, then set the glass down. "I'm a friend of Brenda Evans. Do you know who she is?"

He shrugged. "No."

"She's Sally's mother."

"Oh."

The waitress returned and set a Corona down on the table. He paid for it, then took a gulp.

"Brenda's looking for Sally."

"I haven't seen her."

I contemplated him for a long time. He locked eyes with me defiantly, but I knew he was lying. The music, heavy with bass, pounded in the background. He finally looked away.

"You know where she is," I said.

"Not tonight. I don't know what she's up to."

"Are you living with her?"

He snorted. "No. She's too crazy."

"In what way?"

"I dunno. She's a ditz." He glanced around, searching for a free table, but there weren't any. "Go away."

"Sally recently moved."

"So?"

"Where's her new place?"

He suddenly leaned forward. "I don't know who you are, and I'm not telling you anything."

"Fair enough," I said. "But do this for me. When you see Sally – because I'm sure you will – tell her to get in touch with her family. It's important."

He gazed at me, his expression neutral. "Yeah, sure," he finally said. "I'll do that. Now I'm expecting someone, so beat it."

I searched his face, doubting he would actually deliver the

message to Sally. "Are you seeing her later tonight?"

He glanced away. "No."

Another lie.

He sat back and took a gulp of beer, then set the bottle down with a thump and crossed his arms, letting me know he was through talking. I signaled the waitress and asked for her pen.

"If Sally doesn't want to talk to her family," I said as I took the pen from the waitress, "tell her to call me." I grabbed a napkin on the table and wrote my number on it.

Just then, a man neatly dressed in black slacks and a blue-striped shirt came through the door. Like me, he immediately stuck out like a sore thumb. Gabe glanced at him, then motioned at me to leave.

"My friend is here," he said, "so…" He stuffed the napkin in his pocket without looking at it.

"Right." I got up and walked back to the end of the bar.

The man made his way over to Gabe's table, threw him a polite nod, then sat down where I'd just been. The waitress went over and took his drink order, and then Gabe and his friend began talking. I watched them for a minute as I sipped my Coke. Then I waved at Ella.

"Does Gabe know where Sally is?" she asked.

"He said no, but he's lying."

She pursed her lips, not surprised by my answer.

I jerked my head toward their table. "Do you know who that man is?"

She studied Gabe's friend in the dim light. "He was in here the last time Gabe was, at least if my memory's not letting me down. They were talking, just like that, for quite a while." She stared at them for a moment longer. "He may have been in another time or two, but I can't be sure."

"So you don't know his name."

"Nope."

"Thanks."

She began wiping down the bar, and I took a few pictures of the man with my phone, careful to do it so no one would notice.

The waitress brought the man a Coors, and he took a long drink from it and set it down. I nursed my Coke and watched Gabe and his friend out of the corner of my eye. As the two men talked, they became more animated. The man waved his hands in the air a few times, but the music drowned out their conversation. After a bit, they leaned into the table, their faces close together. Finally, the man reached into his pocket, pulled out something, and slid it across the table. Gabe palmed it and crammed it in his pocket.

A drug exchange? I wondered.

I glanced over at Ella. She'd seen the interaction as well. She came over.

"Drugs?" I said.

She shrugged. "I don't want that in here." She put her hands on the bar and stared at the two men.

They talked for a minute longer, then the man suddenly jammed a finger at Gabe. Gabe shrugged, leaned back, and said something. The man leaped to his feet, almost toppling his beer. The music stopped, and their voices cut into the abrupt silence.

"You think that's the way it works?" he said as he stared down at Gabe. "You don't tell me how to do things. Are you trying to screw this up?"

People at the other tables hardly noticed them.

Gabe laughed. "Cool it, man."

"I should –"

Another song began and swallowed their voices. The man yelled something else, then whirled around and stormed out of the bar. Gabe drained his beer, then got on his phone again.

"What was that about?" I mused.

Ella shrugged. "That's Gabe, always making enemies."

She busied herself again while I kept my eye on Gabe. He appeared to be texting someone. When he finished, he stood up and headed for the door. I signaled Ella and pointed at the door at the end of the bar.

"Can I go out the back way?"

She shrugged. "Sure."

"Thanks."

I hurried through the kitchen and out into the lot at the back of the bar. I slipped around the corner and tiptoed along the side of the building. When I neared the front, I peeked into the street. A man was walking down Steele Street. When he passed under a streetlight, I saw his face.

Gabe.

He crossed the street and got into a dark-colored Ford Tempo. My 4-Runner was parked nearby, and I ran to it. By the time I'd started it and reached the corner, the Tempo was two blocks ahead. I kept my headlights off and followed. The Tempo drove to Colorado Boulevard and turned right. I let Gabe get ahead, then flicked on my headlights and pulled onto Colorado. The street was busy, and it was easy to stay several cars back where Gabe wouldn't notice me. Gabe didn't seem to realize he was being tailed, and he stayed in the left lane until he passed Bruce Randolph Avenue. Then he pulled into a McDonald's.

As I drove past the lot, Gabe was walking inside. I turned at the next street, went around the block, and parked at the other end of the lot from his car. I pulled out binoculars from the back seat and focused through the glass windows. Gabe was standing in line to order. Once he got his meal, he took a seat by the front window, sipped his drink, and waited. A few minutes later, a man wearing jeans and a black hoodie walked up and sat down next to Gabe. I shifted in my seat to get a better look at the man, but I could only see Gabe's face. They talked for a bit, then both got up and left. I still never saw the man's face.

Gabe walked back to his car and drove out of the parking lot, then headed south on Colorado. I tossed the binoculars on the passenger seat and followed. Gabe drove a few miles per hour over the speed limit to Eighteenth Avenue, then went west. Less than a mile later, he turned onto Race Street.

I slowed down as I neared Race and glanced in the rearview mirror. No cars were around, so I flicked off my headlights and turned down the street. The Tempo was halfway down the block. Gabe parallel-parked, and then got out and marched up the sidewalk to a four-story apartment building. He flung open a glass door and disappeared inside.

I headed down the block, found a space near the corner, flipped a U-turn and parked. Now I had a good view of the building. I sat back and waited. A dim light over the door to the apartment building barely illuminated a small porch. A few minutes later, a group of people walked down the street and went into the building. I yawned, and another man hurried inside. Ten minutes passed. Two people emerged from the apartments, walked to an SUV in front of the building, and drove away. I waited. It was now just after eleven. Then a white Hyundai drove up and took the spot where the SUV had been, and a woman with shoulder-length hair got out and walked toward the building. I grabbed my binoculars and trained them on her. As she stepped up to the door, she glanced left and right. When she turned my way, her face was briefly illuminated in the porchlight.

Sally Evans.

She opened the door and went inside.

I exchanged the binoculars for my Glock and ankle holster, which I'd stashed under the seat, then got out. I quickly strapped on the gun and holster, and ran to the apartment building. I yanked open the door and entered a small vestibule that had a set of mailboxes to the left and a pegboard with flyers on the right. In front of me was a glass security door. I tried it but it was locked. I peered inside. Hallways led to the left and right, and a stairwell was opposite the door.

I turned to the mailboxes and scanned them. Each one had a small call button below the box, and each box was labeled. One had "Culpepper" on it. Gabe was in apartment 302. Was Sally living here too, or was she just visiting Gabe? It didn't really matter for my purposes. I just wanted to talk to her, and then I could leave.

I rang the buzzer for Gabe's apartment and waited. When no one buzzed the door, I pressed the button again, this time holding it for an annoyingly long time. Still nothing. I stood for a moment, mulling over my options. Then the outer door opened and a man strolled in. He used a key to let himself through the security door and headed down the hall to the left. Just before the door closed, I pulled it open and slipped inside. The man had already vanished into an apartment.

I took the stairs to the third floor. Somewhere down the hall, music was playing, the sound not nearly as loud as the Rat Tavern. I walked in the opposite direction to 302, then stopped, put my ear to the door and listened.

Silence.

I reached up to knock, but noticed the door was slightly ajar. I pushed it gently and it swung inward. I found myself looking into a small living room with an old couch, a TV stand, and a large desk in the corner. Near the desk was an open window, and a breeze was gently blowing cheap curtains. Sally Evans was bent down at the desk, searching through some papers. I took a few steps into the room, and then I noticed Gabe.

He was lying on the floor on the other side of the couch, and he had a small black hole in his forehead.

CHAPTER SEVEN

I'd found Nightmare Sally – and a whole lot more than I'd bargained for. I quickly reached down and pulled out my Glock, then aimed it at Sally's back.

"Turn around slowly," I ordered her.

She whirled around with a gasp. Then she slowly raised her hands. "I didn't kill him."

I moved farther into the room and looked at Gabe. His eyes stared blankly at the ceiling, and it was clear he was dead. He'd taken off his leather coat and it was draped over the arm of the couch. A small gun lay by his side.

I glanced at Sally. "Did you call the police?"

She shook her head.

"Why not?" I kept my gun on her and pulled out my phone with my other hand.

"I … I was going to …"

I dialed 911 and reported the situation.

"Wait, you're not the police?"

I shook my head, then introduced myself. "Your mother hired me to find you." My eyes darted to Gabe, then back at her. "This wasn't what I expected to find."

"I didn't kill him," she repeated. She stepped away from the desk.

"Stay where you are," I said.

She stopped and sighed. "Can I at least put my arms down?"

I nodded. "Keep your hands where I can see them."

She leaned back against the side of the desk and crossed her arms. She had a glazed look in her eyes, as if she were in shock.

"If you didn't do this," I gestured at the body, "then who?"

She took a second to answer. "I don't know. He was like that when I got here."

"Do you live here?"

She shook her head. "Gabe does. I was just visiting."

"Why didn't you call the police?" I asked again.

She hesitated. "I was looking for something. Then I was going to call them."

"Looking for what?"

"He has some stuff of mine. I figured once the police showed up, I wouldn't be able to get into the apartment. I watch the cop shows on TV. They'll seal up the apartment, and no one can get in. Then I'd never get my stuff back."

"Get what?"

"None of your business."

I gestured at Gabe again. "This doesn't look good for you."

Her lip trembled. "I know."

Through the open window, the sound of sirens drifted in. Sally cocked her head.

"I didn't shoot him," she whispered. "They'll know that, right? My prints aren't on the gun."

"You could've worn gloves."

"I didn't." She stared at me. "What're you doing here?"

"I've been looking for you for a while, and I thought Gabe would lead me to you. Turns out he did."

Her mouth formed a little O. "Why is my mother looking for me? I'm doing all right."

"Not anymore, and let me give you a little advice. Call your parents. They can help you with this situation."

She stared down at the floor and we waited in silence. I was surprised no one else in the building had heard the shot and had come to see what happened. I was also surprised with Sally's reaction, and I didn't know whether to believe her or not. She wasn't crying, and she hadn't called the police. Was she in shock? Or was she a coldblooded murderer?

A few minutes later, a buzz sounded near the door. I backed up, careful to keep my gun on Sally. I needn't have worried because she was still staring at the floor, her shoulders stooped.

I pressed a button near a speaker by the door, then opened it. I poked my head out. Hurried footsteps sounded on the stairs, and a moment later, two uniformed officers entered the hallway.

"Down here," I said, then bent down and holstered my Glock.

They rushed down the hall and through the doorway. One of them cornered me, and I flashed him my PI license. He made me surrender my gun, while the other moved slowly into the apartment. Things happened fast after that. One of them checked Gabe, then called in reinforcements. Sally told the uniforms what she'd told me, and I could tell they were skeptical of her story. They handcuffed her and escorted her from the apartment, then asked me to wait in the hall. Someone came out of an apartment, and the uniforms asked him to go back into his unit. They took Sally outside, and I stood in the hallway while they asked me questions and filled out a report. I explained who I was, showed them the license for my gun, and told them what I knew. By this time, homicide detectives had shown up.

I knew them well. One was Roland Youngfield, better known as "Spats" because he liked to dress well. Another was Ernie Moore, in his typical attire, a rumpled suit, the epitome of the detective cliché. The third – and senior detective – was a tall, blond-haired woman in stylish jeans and a yellow blouse. When she came up the stairs, she saw me and frowned.

"What're you doing here?" she asked.

Detective Sarah Spillman was with Denver Homicide, and she and I had run into each other on several occasions. Over the years, she'd gained a begrudging respect for me, but she was never beyond busting my chops for interfering with her investigations, whether I did or not.

I held up my hands. "It's not what you think."

"It never is," she said.

One of the uniforms eyed us. "You know each other?"

She nodded. "Uh-huh."

"What do we have?" she asked the officer, then glanced at me. "I'll deal with you in a minute."

The three detectives put on latex gloves and booties, then went into the apartment. Spillman then emerged a long time later, took off her gloves and booties, and glanced around. By now, it was just a uniform and me in the hallway.

"What happened?" Spillman asked.

I told her about being hired to find Sally, how I had followed Gabe here, then had seen Sally walk into the building, and what I'd discovered when I entered the apartment.

"That's it?" she asked, her voice laced with skepticism.

On some of my previous cases, I'd occasionally held back information from her, and I couldn't blame her for being doubtful of me.

"I've told you everything," I said, and this time I had.

She thought for a moment. "Okay. Go on home. You can get your gun back after ballistics tests have been run on it."

"What's going to happen to Sally?"

"It doesn't look good for her, does it?"

I shook my head. "No."

She stared at me. "Do you think she did it?"

"I have no idea."

"Hmm," she said.

With that, she went back into the apartment and I left.

CHAPTER EIGHT

It was late when I got home, and Willie was asleep with the kitten snuggled up by her head, so it wasn't until the next morning that I could tell her what had happened. It was almost ten, and we were eating a late breakfast while we talked.

"I'm going to call Brenda, just in case Sally didn't," I said when I finished.

Willie picked up the kitten and started petting it. "She would've called her parents, don't you think?"

I shrugged. "With her, who knows?"

"After so many days looking for Sally, that was an abrupt end to your case," she said wryly.

"Not the way I saw things playing out, that's for sure."

"I'm glad you don't have to keep hanging out at that bar."

"It wasn't so bad. If they'd put in a pool table, that would help."

"But you'd miss your '80s music."

"So true." She rubbed the kitten's ears. "What do you think about Chance for a name?"

"Chance?"

"He's getting a second chance with us."

"You're sure it's a boy?"

She held him up. "I think so. I'll take him to the vet and get him checked out."

"We need to make sure he doesn't have a home," I said.

"I doubt he does." She started in with some baby-talk and kissed his head.

I leaned over the table and stared at the kitten. "How about Bogart? Or Humphrey?"

"Hon, please, be serious."

"I am." I was smiling when my phone rang. I glanced at the number. "It's Brenda Evans."

Willie tipped her head at me. "Her ears must've been burning." She got up from the table. "I'm going to hop in the shower, and then I have some errands to run." She walked out of the room with the kitten at her heels.

I nodded and answered the phone.

"Reed, you've got to help us," Brenda said without any preamble. She spoke fast, in a full panic.

"You've talked to Sally," I said, the Great Detective using his deductive powers.

"Yes. She called early this morning from jail. From jail!" she wailed. "We've been dealing with the police and lawyers ever since. Oh, it's awful."

"Was she charged?"

"Not yet, but she's a solid suspect, that's what they said."

"They didn't charge her?" I was surprised by that.

"They're not able to pin the murder on her just yet because her fingerprints weren't on the gun, and she didn't have any gunshot residue on her hands. From what I can gather, it's all circumstantial evidence at this point. And she denied doing it, so they don't have a confession."

"So the police are building their case against her."

"I would assume so. Sally told me you were there last night, and that you urged her to call us. I'm so glad she took your advice."

"There's not much I can do now."

"There is. I want to hire you to find Gabe's killer."

I hesitated. "What if Sally did it?"

"She didn't. I know her. She may be flaky, but she's not a killer."

You may not know her as well as you think, I mused, but didn't say out loud.

"Can you meet us somewhere so we can talk about this?" she asked.

"Us?"

"Sally and me. Please, I don't know where else to turn."

"Okay, meet me at the Starbucks on the Sixteenth Street Mall. It's near Market Street."

"We can be there in an hour."

"I'll see you then."

I ended the call and went to tell Willie that my case had been reopened. We chatted for a minute, and I left. I went down the stairs on the side of my building, and ran right into Ace and Deuce Smith, my downstairs neighbors. They are fun-loving, pool-playing characters. They aren't, however, the sharpest tools in the drawer, so I'd affectionately dubbed them the Goofball Brothers.

"Hey, Reed," they said in unison. They sound almost alike, and they also look very much alike, with dirty blond hair and light gray eyes. But Deuce is more solidly built, thanks to his construction job, whereas Ace works in the electronics department at Best Buy, and his slight physique shows it.

Deuce had his phone in his hand, and they were laughing about something.

"You on a case?" Ace asked.

"I am," I said.

Deuce's eyebrows shot up. "Need any help?"

Ever since I'd become a private investigator, both brothers, uniquely named because of their father's love of poker, loved to help me on my cases. And sometimes, they did help with stakeouts. But it was a bit like working with Inspector Clouseau, so I had to be careful in the tasks I asked them to do. Deuce desperately wanted to carry a gun, but I didn't see that ever happening.

"Not right now," I said. "But I'll let you know."

Sounds came from Deuce's phone, and Ace started laughing.

I pointed at the phone. "What's so funny?"

"It's this guy who posts these videos," Ace said. "His name is Masta Dig. He's a riot. Here, watch this one."

Deuce held out the phone and I watched a short video. In it a man in a black-and-white mask that had a long face and wide eyebrows over slits for eyes was dancing to a techno beat. Then he looked at the camera and talked about how cool he was. As he did, a big snake began winding up his arm. The video ended with the masked man saying, "Dig it, peace."

"Look at that snake," Deuce said. He really liked snakes.

I stared at the video, then looked at the Goofballs.

"He's funny," Ace said.

"Uh-huh." The humor in the video was lost on me. "I've got to go." I waved goodbye and got out of there before I was subjected to more videos. I could still hear them laughing when I got into my car.

»»»»»

Since I no longer kept a formal office, I liked to meet clients at the Starbucks on Denver's outdoor pedestrian mall. It was easy to find, and being at a coffee shop seemed to put people at ease. When I arrived at eleven, Brenda and Sally were sitting outside at a table with an umbrella. It was warm, the sun shining, with the hint of a breeze; a perfect day, but you never would've known that by looking at the two of them.

Brenda was in a blue pantsuit, sans any gold jewelry. Her already wan face seemed even more drawn than when I'd first seen her. Her makeup was anything but artful, as if she'd hurriedly applied some lipstick and blush, and she had a flowery silk scarf wrapped around her head. Sally was in the same torn jeans and flowered blouse she'd been the night before, but she'd pulled her hair back into a short ponytail, and I was struck by how severe it made her look. Dark circles under her eyes told of a long, sleepless night. Both women were frowning as they pretended to sip their drinks.

"Hello," I said as I came over.

Brenda looked up and managed a small smile, but the frown quickly returned. "Thanks for meeting us. Do you want anything to drink?"

I shook my head and sat down. I'd expected a healthy dose of tension between the two women, and it was there, but they also seemed glad to be around each other, despite the circumstances.

"I don't know where to start," Brenda said.

I turned to Sally. "I need to know about your conversation with the police." I tried to make eye contact with her, but she glanced away. "What did the police say to you about Gabe?"

Sally fiddled with her glass and finally looked at me. "They think I killed him."

"I know that," I said. "Did you?"

"Of course not," Brenda snapped.

I held up a hand. "Let me hear things from Sally, okay?"

Brenda's cheeks turned red, and she murmured an apology. I turned to Sally, and we spoke in low tones so that people at the other tables wouldn't hear us.

"Did you?" I repeated to Sally.

She shook her head. "I told you last night, I told the police over and over again, and I'll tell you now, I did *not* kill Gabe."

I searched her face. If she was lying, she knew how to cover it well. For the moment, I would have to take her word for it.

"If not you, then who?"

She shrugged. "I have no idea."

"From what your mother told me, it sounds like the case against you is largely circumstantial."

Sally nodded. "Since I never touched the gun, they won't be able to prove I fired it."

"But you were there, and you didn't even call the police to tell them about Gabe."

She looked miserable. "I know it looks bad."

"Honey, we'll get through this," Brenda murmured.

Sally nodded.

I leaned forward. "Let's move beyond how it looks. Do the police think you have a motive for killing him?"

"I don't know," Sally said. "I didn't tell them anything."

"Anything?"

"I told them exactly what I told you, that I went to Gabe's to get some things that belonged to me. I found him there, already dead, but I knew if they sealed up his apartment, I'd probably never get my stuff back. I was going to find my stuff and then call the police."

"What stuff?"

"Just … some things of mine. You'll think it's silly."

Brenda reached out and put her hand on Sally's arm. "You need to be honest with Reed, so he can help."

Sally looked at her mother sadly, then finally nodded. "He had some notebooks and files of mine, with poetry and lyrics, things like that. And some journals. That's why I went over there, to get them back. He's had them for a while because he was helping scan them so I could save them on my computer. But every time I asked for them, he'd make up some excuse about why he wouldn't give them back to me. Last night, I thought he was gone, and I let myself in with a key. I was going to get them and be gone. But it didn't turn out that way."

"That sounds pretty lame," I said.

Her chin went up. "It's the truth."

"Okay. Did you check Gabe to see if he was dead?"

"Um." For the first time, her composure wavered, and her eyes watered. "I was so shocked, I just stood there for a moment. I remember taking a deep breath, and it sounded so loud in the room. Then I pulled out my phone and started to dial, and that's when it hit me that I should find my stuff first."

"So you left him there."

She nodded. "I … tried not to look at him."

"You told the police that?"

Her head dropped in shame. "Yes."

That didn't look good, I thought. "What else did the police ask you?"

"They wanted to know if Gabe and I were a couple."

"Were you?"

She hesitated, then looked up. "Yes."

I stared at her. "What?"

"I think Gabe was seeing other people."

"He was cheating on you." It was blunt, but now wasn't the time for subtleties.

She bit her lip. "Yes."

"Were you jealous of that?"

"Maybe."

"Did you tell the police this?"

"Um, maybe."

"Sally," I said slowly.

She kept gnawing her lip. "I don't think I told them that."

"They might think your jealousy is a motive," I said. "What else did they ask you about Gabe?"

"If we fought, did anyone see us fighting, what did we fight about."

"And you told them yes to all that?"

"Well," she glanced uncomfortably at her mother, and then her jaw dropped.

It had suddenly dawned on her what answering my questions meant.

"Oh, god." She ran a hand over her face. "The police will think because Gabe and I sometimes fought, or if I was jealous, that's why I wanted to kill him?"

I nodded.

"But ... people fight," she said. "That doesn't mean they'll commit murder!"

Her voice had risen, and a woman at another table glanced at us. Sally gulped and then leaned closer to the table.

"These days, people don't need much for a motive," I said.

"I didn't do it!" she hissed.

I ignored that. Her protestations wouldn't do us any good.

I put my elbows on the table. "Did you talk about any other motive?"

She thought for a second. "They asked if Gabe owed me any money, and he doesn't. They wanted to know if anyone knew I was going to his place last night, and if anyone saw me go into his apartment."

"Did anyone?"

She shook her head. "The hall was quiet. I don't think anyone was around."

"Anything else?"

"That was about it. By that point, I kept telling them I was innocent, and that they should look for the guy in the alley."

I jerked up. "What guy in the alley?"

"When I was over by the desk, I heard a noise outside the window. I went over and looked out, and someone was at the bottom of the fire escape. He dropped to the ground and ran off."

"He?"

"I assume it was a man, but it could've been a woman. It was dark, and all I saw was someone in a dark-colored hoodie."

"Did you tell the police this?"

"Of course. I'm not sure they believed me."

"Was that person in the apartment?"

"I don't know."

"They'll at least look for that person," I said, "and anyone else who might've heard or seen something."

She sighed. "I don't think they'll find anything."

I gave her a hard look. "They're going to investigate you as well, so you need to tell me if there's anything bad that they'll uncover, any skeletons in your closet."

Her eyes darted toward her mother. "Like what?" Sally asked.

"Have you ever been arrested?"

"A long time ago, for public indecency."

Brenda's lips twitched, but she managed to stay quiet.

I kept my gaze on Sally. "What else?"

"That's it. No other arrests."

"What other kinds of things? Have your neighbors heard you fighting with anyone besides Gabe?"

"No."

I tapped the table, thinking. "They'll be looking at banking and credit card statements."

"I only have a couple of cards, and there's nothing on them that would incriminate me."

"Did you recently buy gloves of any kind?"

"Of course not. Oh." She pursed her lips. "I see what you mean."

"What?" Brenda asked.

I pointed at Sally. "If she's bought anything that might've been used while she allegedly murdered Gabe, the police will find it, and I need to know about it."

Brenda nodded. "Right." Then she looked at Sally. "Well?"

"There *isn't* anything," Sally said.

"Do you own any guns?" I asked.

She shook her head. "No. I don't know who owned that gun at Gabe's. He didn't have any guns that I'm aware of."

I thought for a moment, then pulled out a pad and pen. "Where do you work?"

"Jones Transportation, as a receptionist." She gave me the address.

"How long have you been there?"

"A month. I've done some temp work there off and on, in the past."

I nodded. "Where are you living now?"

"Over on Humboldt." She rattled off an address near Cheesman Park. "My roommate's named Kristen Dalrymple."

"What's her number?"

She pulled out her phone. "I can't remember anyone's number. I have to look it up." She tapped the screen, then gave me Kristen's number.

I jotted down all of it. "I'm going to ask around, see what people tell me about you, so you might want to let them know."

Sally gulped. "I understand, but you won't find anything bad."

"Okay, I believe you," I said, mostly to keep her as relaxed as possible. I glanced at Brenda. "Would you mind if I talked to Sally privately for a few minutes?"

Brenda's eyes widened in surprise, but then she nodded. She pulled a check from her purse and handed it to me. "This should cover a week."

"That's fine," I said.

I had her sign some paperwork and put it into the padfolio I'd brought with me.

"Thank you," Brenda said.

I nodded. "I'll be in touch as soon as I find out anything."

"Thank you." Brenda stood up, then gestured toward the mall. "I'll take a little walk. The air will do me good. Sally, call me when you're finished."

"Okay," Sally said.

Brenda walked away, and Sally fiddled with her drink and shifted in her seat, seeming desperate to leave with Brenda.

CHAPTER NINE

"Why'd you ask my mother to leave?" Sally asked.

"I figured you might be more comfortable answering some questions without her around."

She gave me a faint smile of appreciation. "There's a lot she doesn't know about me."

I let the comment linger for a moment, then said, "What was your relationship with Gabe really like?"

She took a sip of her drink, grimaced, and set it down. "We fought, and a time or two it came to blows, but only those times."

"Because he was cheating on you."

"Yeah."

I remembered what Ella had said, about Gabe showing up with marks on his face. "Did you hit him?"

"Once, I threw a book at him. Hit him right in the side of the face and gave him a black eye. And another time I clawed him pretty good."

"Only those times?"

"Yes. He hit me sometimes, too. I don't know why I put up with it, but …" Her voice faded.

"And you told the police all this? In detail?"

"Yeah." She frowned. "I didn't think it mattered, but it will to the police, right?"

"Like I said, they need a motive." She started to protest, but I held up a hand. "Let's focus on Gabe. He was a bit younger than you?"

She glared at me. "You judging me?"

"Nope. Just trying to find out as much as I can about him and hope that leads me to his murderer."

"Oh. He was twenty-one."

I went on. "What'd you see in him?"

She thought about that. "He was cute, and it was fun to go clubbing with him. That's where I met him, at Club 77. He was a good dancer, and a great deejay. But mostly it was about music." She was visibly relaxing. "We liked the same bands, and we could talk about that for hours. Not just 'that's a good song' or 'it's got a good beat,' but we really *talked* about the music, you know? Stuff like how they used different instruments to get a certain feel, or how the lyrics were. Gabe was a musician, too, like me."

"Your mother didn't mention you played an instrument."

"Just guitar. I picked it up along the way." She laughed. "I did play piano growing up – didn't everyone? But it didn't stick. I like the guitar, and I write songs."

"Did Gabe write any songs?"

Now she snorted. "He couldn't write lyrics, but he was a helluva techno musician."

"Techno musician?" I'd heard plenty of techno – repetitive dance music with an electronic sound that rarely had lyrics – because it had been played at dance clubs that I'd been in … back in the days when I'd gone to dance clubs. But I knew little of what went into creating the sound.

"Yeah, these days you don't need a studio or a band to produce techno," she said. "You can create all kinds of stuff with just your computer and a software program. People upload songs on YouTube and Spotify, and boom – you become a hit." She shrugged. "Or some people do. I've never had that kind of luck."

"You've uploaded songs to the Internet?"

"Yeah, but they never seem to find an audience."

"How else would you find an audience?"

"Playing clubs, although there aren't that many good ones around here. I tried L.A., and I had a little bit of success there, but it didn't last. It's a tough scene. Then there's all the Internet stuff, like having a website and being on social media. But I don't really do social media, and I don't have a website."

"Why not?"

"Social media became a distraction for me; I spent too much time on it, and not actually working on my music. And a website's too expensive."

I thought about all the free sites and blogs that one could use to set up and host a website, but I didn't point that out. They weren't always the slickest sites, but in a pinch, they would do. I moved on. I wondered how motivated she really was.

"And you shared your lyrics and stuff with Gabe, but he wouldn't give it all back."

"Right," she said. "I write a lot of stuff down in notebooks."

"Why'd he keep them?"

She sighed. "We weren't really seeing each other much by then, and he was being a jerk, being difficult just to piss me off."

"You think he was stealing your lyrics?"

She laughed and shook her head. "He was just helping scan it. That way, I could have the files on my computer, in case anything happened to my notebooks."

"So, other than his keeping your notebooks, you thought Gabe was nice?" I couldn't keep the skepticism from my voice.

"I guess so."

I stared hard at her. "That doesn't sound convincing."

"To answer your question, Gabe could be nice, when he wanted to. But if you got on his wrong side, look out."

"What'd you fight about?"

"Usually his cheating on me. Sometimes money. Or he'd be hung over and he'd pick a fight about who knows what. I put up with it because I thought he loved me, but then I realized he didn't, and he was just using me."

"For what?"

Her lips twitched into a sly smile. "I'm pretty good in bed, if you know what I mean. He liked that. And he was good, too."

"Okay." I deftly moved on. "Did you love him?"

"At first, maybe. Not at the end."

"And once you realized he didn't love you, you stayed with him only because of the music?"

"Why else?"

"I'm asking you."

She cleared her throat. "I know I should've left him, but he was helping me produce stuff. And he did help with the rent, now and again."

"Why'd you move out of the apartment on Columbine?"

"The rent got too high."

"How'd you meet Kristen?"

"Clubbing. It seemed like we just kept running into each other, and we hit it off. She's really cool."

I thought for a moment. "Enemies may be too strong a word, but did you know of anyone who disliked Gabe?"

She snorted. "Lots of people didn't like him."

"Why?"

"Because he's arrogant and thinks he knows everything."

"Was there anyone in particular that you can think of?"

"He used to be friends with a guy named Davon, spelled with an 'a,' but they had some kind of fight, and I haven't seen Davon around in a while. I don't think Gabe talks to him anymore."

"What's a while?"

"A couple of months, maybe."

"What's Davon's last name?"

"I don't know."

"What was their fight about?"

"I'm not sure. The last time I saw Gabe and Davon together, Gabe was saying something about he didn't want that action with Davon anymore. That made Davon mad, and they argued about it."

"What kind of action was Gabe talking about?"

"I don't know," she repeated.

"You heard the conversation but you don't remember what it was about?"

"I went on the dance floor."

"I see." I mulled that over. "Did Gabe do drugs, or deal?"

"We smoked a little weed, but I don't think he did anything else. And he didn't deal drugs, at least not around me."

"Then it's still possible he was a dealer, he just kept it from you."

She nodded. "Yeah."

"Ella at the Rat told me Gabe didn't have a job."

Her eyebrows raised. "You've been there?"

I nodded. "I spent more time there than I'd like, hoping that Gabe would come around and lead me to you."

"He did."

"Yep."

Her lips twisted up. "Count Ella as one who didn't like Gabe."

"So I gathered. But she does like you."

That brought a smile. "Ella's a nice lady. She's been through the wringer. A rough upbringing, a bad marriage, and who knows what else. But she's made a living with that bar, and she likes to help people out."

"She said she gave you a lot of chances, but …"

"Yeah. I just couldn't seem to keep track of everyone's orders, and sometimes Gabe and I would be working on our music, partying a bit, and I'd forget to go in."

"What about the job you're at now? You're making a go of it?"

"So far." She shrugged. "I need to."

I went back to Gabe. "Did he work?"

"He got some deejay gigs, mostly at Club 77. That's a place on Evans, near Colorado."

It was in the same area where I'd gone clubbing, a long time ago. I wrote it down. "But no steady work?"

She shook her head.

"Gabe met with a guy at the Rat last night before he came home." I showed her the picture I'd taken at the Rat Tavern. "Do you know him?"

She thought long and hard. "He seems familiar, but where was that?" She finally snapped her fingers. "He showed up at Club 77 one time, but I can't come up with a name."

"What do you know about him?"

"Nothing, just that he and Gabe went outside the club and talked for quite a while."

"About what?"

She shrugged. "Beats me. Gabe wouldn't tell me anything about that guy, or what they discussed."

"Before he left the Rat the other night, he got mad at Gabe."

"Gabe pissed somebody else off, big surprise."

I rubbed my jaw for a moment. "It sounds like Gabe was a real charmer."

"Sarcasm, ha ha. Yeah, Gabe wasn't very popular."

"Is there anything else you can tell me about this man at the club?"

She pursed her lips, thinking. "I think the owner of Club 77 knew him because Gabe and that man had a long conversation with the owner that same night. Then they all shook hands before the man left."

"I can talk to the owner to see what he'll tell me about this man," I said. "Do you know the bar owner's name?"

She shook her head. "Sam, but I don't know his last name, either."

Of course not. I resisted sighing. "Did you ever meet Gabe's family?"

"He has an older sister, Lisa, that I met at the clubs. She was kind of fun to hang around. I never met his parents."

"Did Lisa ever talk to you about Gabe?"

"Not really. She couldn't understand why I was with him, either." She threw me a rueful smile. "I was just hoping he might be able to help me out with my music."

"Do you know any of his neighbors?"

"Just the guy next door, in 303. Luis. He came over a time or two when I was at Gabe's. He's an okay guy."

I went over our conversation, but I couldn't think of anything else to ask right then. I had a list of people to talk to about Gabe, and I hoped that one of them might have an idea of who would want him dead.

Sally stared at me. "Well?"

"Do you have a cell phone, in case I need to get hold of you?"

"Yeah, it's a cheap disposable one. I lost my other phone and I hadn't paid the bill anyway, so the number's disconnected."

"Give me the new number."

She did and I entered it into my phone. "But I'm warning you, I don't always keep my phone with me."

"You need to now."

She sighed. "Okay."

I studied her for a moment. "May I throw out a bit of advice to you?"

She sat back and crossed her arms. "Are you going to lecture me?"

"Maybe." I held up my hands. "Look, I get wanting to pursue your dreams."

"Really?"

"Yes. My parents wanted me to be a lawyer or go into finance. I flitted around from job to job, until I finally decided that I wanted to be a private investigator, and I've pursued this career. It hasn't always been easy, and it takes a lot of hard work and commitment."

"Nothing comes easy."

"Not usually, and that's my point. You don't need to rely on a Gabe to get what you want. Rely on yourself. You said yourself that nowadays anyone can produce music and put it up on the internet, so you can, too."

"Nice pep talk."

"Okay, sorry," I said. "One final thing."

She sighed dramatically.

"You don't have to abandon your family and friends in the process."

She glanced toward the mall and her lip trembled. "My mother's not doing well."

"I know. You may not have a lot of time with her. Make the most of it."

She looked at me and blinked hard. "I hear you. I've missed a lot of time with her."

She may have been acting like a ditz, but I suddenly felt sad for her. She'd made some bad choices, but that didn't make her a bad person.

"Okay, I've peppered you with enough questions for now." I put my notepad away. "If I think of anything else, I'll call you."

She reached out and touched my arm in the same manner her mother had. "I know you must think I'm flaky, that I don't have my crap together, and all that may be true, but I didn't kill Gabe. Please, find whoever did. I don't want to go to prison."

"I'll do my best to uncover the truth."

She gazed at me and nodded. "I'll take that."

I stood up. "I'll be in touch soon."

I turned around and walked away. When I got to the corner, I glanced back. Sally was still at the table, staring into space.

I'd found out a lot about her, and I wasn't sure I bought her reasoning for being in Gabe's apartment when he'd been killed. But did that mean she was guilty?

I'd find out soon enough.

CHAPTER TEN

Sally had given me two people that would be worth talking to: Davon and the man I'd seen with Gabe Culpepper at the Rat Tavern. The problem was, could I find them? And did either have anything to do with Gabe's death? When I'd seen Gabe and his friend at the Rat on Sunday night, the man had said something about Gabe screwing things up, but did that mean anything? Had he been angry enough to kill Gabe?

By now, I'd reached the 4-Runner. I got in and thought for a moment. I really needed to know what the police had on Sally, and I knew who would tell me as much as she could. I pulled out my phone and dialed Spillman.

"Please tell me you're not working on the Evans case," she said when she answered. She'd greeted me other times with similar words.

"Okay." I let the silence stretch out between us.

"Ferguson?"

"Yes?"

"What do you want?"

"Well, I'm working on the Evans case, but you didn't want me to tell you that."

"Smartass."

"I try."

A long, put-upon breath sounded through the phone. "I suppose you want to talk about the case."

"Anything you can share would be helpful. After all, if Sally's innocent, you want to find the real killer."

"Meet me at the Rooster & Moon in an hour," she said, and then she was gone.

I hung up, started the car, and drove away.

» » » » »

The Rooster & Moon Coffee Pub is a hip little coffee shop on Bannock, in the Golden Triangle neighborhood just south of downtown. It also happened to be near Spillman's precinct, and I'd met her there on occasion. I'd arrived early, and Spillman wasn't there yet. I went inside, and although I was tempted by their sandwiches, I'd had a late breakfast, so I skipped food and ordered a macchiato. I took my drink, which was served in a heavy white mug, went outside, and sat at a table on a long porch.

One of the things I like about the Rooster & Moon is that they play a lot of '80s music, and as I waited for Spillman, "Who Can It Be Now?" by Men at Work played. I listened and enjoyed the sunshine, then pulled out my phone and called Cal.

"What's up?" he said, dispensing with his usual greeting. That meant he was busy.

"My case has taken an interesting turn," I said, then filled him in on Gabe's murder and Sally's potential involvement in it. "Just a quick thing when you have time. I want to know everything you can find on Gabe Culpepper. Check his family, his background and financials, that kind of thing."

"I can do that, but I've got to wrap up a few things first."

"No problem, I appreciate the help."

"I'll get back to you on Gabe."

"Thanks."

I ended the call and then called Sally's roommate Kristen Dalrymple.

"Hello?" a soft voice said.

I told her who I was. "You've heard about Sally?"

"Yes, she called me this morning. She's been with her mother since she left the police department."

"I'd like to talk to you about her."

"Uh, sure, she said you might call. But when? I kinda got a busy day."

I glanced at my watch. "How about around one?" I figured that would give me enough time to talk to Spillman first.

"Um, okay. Can you meet me at Cheesman Park? I can meet you at Franklin Street, where it intersects with the road around the park."

"Sure, I know where you mean." I figured she wanted to meet somewhere public, and I admired her for being careful.

"Okay, I'll see you then." She said goodbye and was gone.

I sat back, sipped my drink, listened to the music, and waited.

Exactly one hour from when I'd talked to Spillman, she showed up. In her tan slacks and red striped blouse, she didn't look like a police detective – until you saw the gun in a holster on her right hip. She strolled up to the table and sat down.

"May I buy you a cup of coffee?" I asked.

"I'll take an espresso," she said.

Her voice sounded tired. She took off her sunglasses and exposed red-rimmed eyes that she quickly rubbed.

"Sure thing," I said.

I went inside, ordered her drink, and when I returned, she was on her phone. I set her mug down in front of her and she mouthed a "thank you," and continued talking on the phone. I tried to glean something from the conversation, hoping it had to do with my case, but she spoke in cryptic terms that meant nothing to me. She finished and slipped her phone in her pocket. Then she picked up her mug, took a sip, and her face relaxed visibly.

"Oh, that's good," she said.

"Long night?"

She held up the mug. "I'd shoot this in my veins if I could."

I laughed. She took another sip, then held the mug in her hands and looked at me, waiting for me to begin the conversation.

"What can you tell me about the crime scene?" I asked. "I've got some information from Sally, but I'd like to hear what you have."

She thought long and hard about how to answer. "I suppose if I don't tell you, you'll find another way to get answers."

I grinned. "I'm resourceful."

"That's what I'm afraid of."

I waited.

"Gabe Culpepper was killed with a Glock 19, a very common handgun, one shot to the head," she said. "As you saw last night, that gun was lying beside him. It had only been fired the one time."

"Who was the gun registered to?"

"It belonged to a man named Anthony Lombardi, but he reported it stolen over a year ago."

"Sally's prints weren't on the gun?"

"No, but there were no traces of any prints at all because it had been wiped clean, and she could've done that."

"You don't know for sure she cleaned off the gun, though."

"The only way I'd know that is if she admitted it, and she didn't."

"So someone else could've done that."

She took a sip, then nodded. "It's possible. Or Sally could've worn gloves."

"But she didn't have any on her, right?"

"No. And we didn't find any in Gabe's apartment."

I eyed her. "And you looked outside the window, too, and elsewhere."

"Yes. No gloves. But that doesn't clear her."

"I know that."

"Her prints were around the apartment."

I rolled my eyes at her. "She was dating Gabe, so of course her prints were there."

"Just testing you."

My mug was almost empty, and I took a big gulp. "Does Sally own a gun?"

She shook her head. "Not legally, anyway."

"Sally said Gabe had some of her notebooks with poetry and song lyrics, and some journals."

"There were some notebooks hidden in some boxes in the bedroom closet."

"She was trying to get them back."

"So she said. After the investigation is over, she can talk to Gabe's family or whoever clears out the apartment, so she can get them back."

I nodded. "Did anyone see her come or go? Besides me."

Two women in shorts walked by. They were talking and laughing, but they must've seen Spillman's gun because they suddenly eyed us warily and their voices dropped to whispers. Spillman pretended as if she hadn't noticed that, but her glance in their direction gave her away. Then she looked back at me and shook her head.

"No one saw or heard anything," she said.

"No one heard the shot?"

"The neighbors close to Gabe weren't home. A woman in the apartment at the other end of the hall heard a pop, but she thought it was from the TV. No one else heard it."

I cocked an eyebrow. "Really? No one else?"

She shrugged. "That's what they say."

"It's not the best neighborhood."

"And?"

"Maybe no one wanted to tell the cops anything."

"It's possible. It seems like people don't want to get involved."

"Sally told you about a man she saw outside the window."

"We canvassed the building, but no one saw a man in the alley last night."

I stared at her. "You think Sally's lying about that?"

She looked down her nose at me. "It wouldn't surprise me."

"Me, either," I said. I moved on. "Sally told me she's only been arrested for public indecency."

"That's correct."

"Anything else in her background I should be aware of?"

She shook her head. "She's stayed out of trouble with the law. Other than that, I don't know yet."

"What about Gabe?"

"He's got a record for assault."

"Interesting. I've heard he's not a popular guy."

She shrugged.

"Do you have any other suspects?"

"We found a piece of paper with your number on it in his pocket."

"I told you last night, I gave that to him at the Rat Tavern."

"Yes, you did."

"You can't believe I'm a suspect," I said indignantly.

She threw me an amused smile. "No."

"Any *other* suspects?"

"No, but we're looking." She gestured at me with her mug. "And obviously you are, too. Do you have any leads?

"Sally said that Gabe had a falling out with a man named Davon." I spelled the name for her.

"Last name?"

I shrugged. "I haven't got that far."

She cocked an eyebrow at me, and I held up my hands.

"It's the truth," I said. "And you remember I told you last night about seeing Gabe at the bar?"

She nodded.

"I don't have a name for him at all."

She pursed her lips. "Sally told you about these two men, that they might be important to our investigation?"

"Yes, what little she knew."

"Let me know if you find more about either one," she finally said. "I'd like to talk to them."

I finished my drink and set my mug down. Then I gazed at her. "What's your gut? Did she do it?"

She drew in a deep breath and let it out slowly. "She's adamant that she's innocent, but I've heard that before."

"And?"

She was very measured in her response. "At this point, I don't know if I believe her or not."

"Neither do I."

"You may find out she did it."

"I'm aware of that," I said. "I appreciate your talking to me."

Her lips formed the faintest of smiles. "I know you well enough to know your motives are pure."

"Thank you."

She nodded, then glanced around. "Did you know the Rooster is closing?"

"Really? I thought it was pretty popular."

"It is." She frowned. "The neighborhood's changed, though, and I think the owners are ready to move on." She let out a sigh. "But I'll miss it. It's a nice place to come and get away from it all." Her head moved with the beat of "Modern Love" by David Bowie. "Man, that's a good song."

I'd never seen this side of her before, and her vulnerability was kind of freaking me out. "It's definitely not Starbucks," I said.

"You got that right." She pushed back her chair and stood up. "I've got to go."

"Crime never sleeps."

"You got that right, too." She chuckled. "Let me know if you find anything."

"I will."

I watched as she walked down Bannock Street and disappeared.

CHAPTER ELEVEN

I left the Rooster, drove to Cheesman Park, and parked on Vine Street, the road that looped through the park. Even though fall was soon to arrive, it was hot, and I was sweating as I walked to Franklin Street and waited on the corner. The park is surrounded by numerous high-rise apartments and condominiums, and the eighty-acre park was bustling with people, some walking, some lounging in the grass, a few eating lunch. One o'clock came and went. Kristen Dalrymple was late.

I had a fleeting thought that maybe she was as flaky as Sally, and then I saw a petite woman strolling down Franklin Street. She looked to be in her early twenties, and she was walking three dogs, a German Shepherd, an Akita, and some kind of Golden Retriever mix. Was she afraid of me, and this was her protection? She approached, holding four leashes tightly. Then, amidst the legs of the other dogs, I spotted a Dachshund. Kristen approached, the dogs in front of her, the little Dachshund trying not to get stepped on.

"Are you Reed?" she asked in a soft voice.

"Yes."

I reached out to shake her hand. She then shifted the dog leashes to her left hand, then reached out and shook mine. Her grip was surprisingly strong.

"Thanks for meeting me," I said, then glanced at the dogs.

She gestured into the park with her free hand, then started walking. "This is one of my jobs," she explained. "I figured I could take care of this and talk to you at the same time."

"No problem." And use the dogs for safety, I thought, but didn't say.

"Sorry I'm late," she said as we crossed the road. "It took me longer to get the dogs than I thought."

We went into the main part of the park and walked through the grass. The dogs seemed to be well-trained, although the German Shepherd had a tendency to pull at his leash, especially when someone passed closer to us.

"Where'd you meet Sally?" I began after a minute of walking.

"Clubbing. We seemed to be at the same places all the time, and we started talking and hanging out."

That fit with what Sally had said. "Tell me about her."

She raked a hand nervously through long red hair that fell around her shoulders. "She's nice enough."

Was I going to have to drag information out of her? "How long have you been roommates?"

"Roommates? Is that what she said?"

I nodded.

That got her going. "We're not roommates. I've got a teeny little basement apartment on Humboldt. I'm just letting Sally crash on my couch for a while until she can get some money saved and get a place of her own."

"That's nice of you."

She stared ahead, then nodded. "I kinda feel sorry for her."

"Why?"

"I dunno. She seems kinda lost to me. She dropped out of college to pursue a music career that never went anywhere, and she's dated the wrong kind of men. She doesn't have any money, she can't keep a job, and she's realizing her life is kinda screwed up."

"I thought she was still pursuing the music."

"Yeah, but for the first time since I've known her, she's talking like maybe she's ready to move on. Or at least get some steady work and a place of her own. And she can pursue the music on the side."

"Have you heard her perform or heard her songs?"

"Uh-huh. It's okay. She writes some pretty good lyrics. But it's not really my style."

"Why not?"

"It's too mellow."

We stopped so the Akita could do his business, and Kristen picked up his poop in a little bag. Then the retriever decided he needed to relieve himself.

"Here, hold this."

Before I could protest, Kristen handed me the bag. I held the bag away from me while she waited on the retriever. This was not where I pictured myself an hour ago. The retriever finished and she bagged up his gift, then finally took the Akita's bag from me. We continued walking, the bags dangling from her free hand. I hoped we'd see a trash can soon.

"Anyway," she went on, "I think Sally should publish some of her poetry. I like it. And she writes some funny stuff, too. I tell her that, but she doesn't seem to want to."

"She's funny?" I asked.

"Oh, yeah, she can really crack you up. Sometimes I think she missed her calling and she should be a comedian, especially if she made fun of herself and the silly things she does."

"Huh. I haven't seen that side of her. Does she have a temper?"

"No, she pretty much goes with the flow and doesn't get angry about stuff."

I turned the conversation in a different direction. "What do you know about Gabe Culpepper?"

Her face scrunched up. "He was an ass."

"How so?"

"He thinks – thought – because he was a deejay and he was producing some music, that he was the bomb, but he wasn't. He was always bragging about how his music was going to hit it big, but I've never seen that."

"Wasn't Gabe helping Sally produce some songs?"

"I don't know about that, but he was doing some videos with another guy."

"Who?"

She shrugged. "I don't know, but Gabe said it was taking off."

"What'd you think of his music?"

"The techno stuff was okay. He posted things on his Facebook page, so you can listen to it if you want to."

"I'll do that," I said.

She sighed. "I'm thinking about Gabe." She shook her head. "I don't wanna speak bad about him, but I don't know what Sally saw in him."

"Did you ever see them fighting?"

A sad look crossed her face. "Yeah. He hit her a time or two, and ripped on her, cussing her out and stuff like that. And he'd mock her by calling her Nightmare Sally."

"I've heard that nickname."

"I guess someone at the Rat came up with that and Gabe would throw it in her face, but I thought that was mean of him. Sally's ditsy, but she's smart, too."

"Did she ever threaten Gabe?"

"Not that I heard or saw."

A man with a big mutt with black fur walked by, and the Dachshund yapped loudly. She scolded it, and he shut up. But the Shepherd pulled hard at the leash. Kristen told him to heel, but he kept tugging. She suddenly stopped and snapped at him in a commanding voice to sit. All four dogs stopped and sat down.

"Sorry," she said to me. She waited a moment, and then started walking again. The dogs fell in line. "The dogs are pretty good overall, but Samson here can be a butthead."

I assumed Samson was the German Shepherd. He seemed oblivious to her name-calling, and trotted along happily.

"Who would want to kill Gabe?"

"Everybody." She let out a wry laugh. "I don't mean that, but I don't know very many people that liked him. Maybe he pissed someone off."

"Over what?"

She shrugged. "I don't know."

"From what you know of Sally, do you think she could've murdered him?"

"No."

"Does Sally own a gun or know how to shoot one?"

Her steps slowed.

"What?" I said.

"A while back, I decided to get a gun, you know, for safety." She waved a hand around. "I have to walk to and from my car, sometimes late at night. I don't always feel safe." She bit her lip.

"And?"

"I go to the range with my father to practice. Sally's gone with me a few times."

"I see. Is she a good shot?"

She nodded.

"Does she own a gun?" I asked again.

"Not that I'm aware of."

"What gun range?"

"The Silver Bullet Shooting Range."

I knew it because I'd been there many times myself, practicing with my Glock. I'd honed my skills over the years, and I was a pretty good shot. I knew some of the men that worked at the Silver Bullet, and I could ask them if they remembered Sally being there.

Kristen stopped and ordered the dogs to sit. Then she stared at me. "Look, her going with me to the gun range might look bad, but I don't think she'd kill *anyone*, let alone Gabe."

"Did you see her at all last night?"

"Unh-uh. I had classes yesterday afternoon, and then I worked my bar job until closing. I didn't get home until after one this morning."

We started walking again.

"Were you surprised that Sally didn't come home last night?" I asked.

She shook her head. "That's not uncommon. She'd stay at Gabe's, or maybe somewhere else."

"With another guy?"

She shrugged. "Maybe."

"Any names?"

"Of guys she was sleeping with? I only know of Gabe."

She spotted a trash can and we veered toward it. She tossed the bags in, then gestured with her now free hand, and we moved on.

"Do you know of a man named Davon?" I asked.

"Sure, I've seen him around."

"What's his last name?"

"I don't know, but I think he works at CJ's. It's some kind of auto repair place. He's a mechanic."

"How well do you know him?"

"Just clubbing with Sally and Gabe. Davon's another one that Gabe pissed off."

"Why?"

She shrugged. "But Davon told me the other day that he'd had it with Gabe."

"Where does Sally work?"

"Jones Transportation."

That's what Sally had told me.

"How long has she been there?" I asked.

"I don't know," she said. "A month or so. I hope she can make it work. I'm happy to help her out, but she can't stay with me forever. I'm in school, and I've got a few part-time jobs to help pay the bills. And my parents are helping me out some, but I don't think they'd be too happy to know I have someone living there. They want me to focus on getting my degree."

We'd made our way to the road and I took that as a signal that Kristen was through talking to me. She stopped and shielded her eyes against the sun as she stared at me.

"Is there anything else you can think of that might help me find Gabe's killer?" I asked.

She thought for a second, then shrugged. "No."

I took out a business card and handed it to her. "If you think of something, give me a call."

She took the card, read it, then handed it back. "You called me, so I've got your number in my phone."

"Ah, right." I took the card back.

"Hey, I've got to get going," she said. "Do you need anything else?"

"Not right now. I appreciate your taking the time to talk to me."

"Sure thing." She bent down and petted the dogs, frowning, then straightened up and looked at me. "I want to help Sally. I know she didn't do that to Gabe."

I thanked her, and watched as she struck a fast pace across the road, the dogs trotting right with her, the Dachshund trying not to get lost in the other dogs' legs. I waited until she disappeared behind some trees, then turned and headed north to where I'd parked.

CHAPTER TWELVE

On the way, I called Sally. She had lied to me about her roommate situation, and about going to the gun range, and I wasn't happy about that. After four rings, the call went to a generic voicemail. I left a message asking her to call me right away, then ended the call, but I was still irritated.

I was now hungry. I spotted a Subway and stopped to have a sandwich and to think through my game plan. I wanted to stop by Gabe's apartment building. If Sally had been telling the truth, and she had seen someone in a hoodie climb down the fire escape when she had been in Gabe's apartment, it was possible another resident in the building might've seen the same person, but not have told the police. I knew Spillman hadn't been happy that I'd said that people might not trust the police, but that was a reality.

I also wanted to find out more about the man I'd seen at the Rat Tavern with Gabe. And finally, I wanted to talk to Davon – if he'd speak with me – to hear about his dispute with Gabe, and to see if that pointed to his being a suspect. Talking to Davon seemed the most prudent option right now, so while I ate my meatball sub, I looked up CJ's auto repair on my phone. It was located not far from where I was, north of downtown. I decided to go there first, and then drop by Gabe's apartment building. After that, I'd see if I could track down the man from the Rat.

I finished my lunch, left the restaurant, and headed up Downing Street. I soon turned right on Thirty-sixth Avenue, and I found CJ's Auto Repair on Lawrence Street. The shop was in a small white building with artful graffiti on the walls. I parked down the block, walked back to the shop, and crossed through their front lot, which was filled with cars, none of them high-end. On the north end of the building were two garage bays with the doors open. The sounds of metal clinking on metal, rock music, and the high-pitched whine of a pneumatic impact air wrench filled the lot.

To the left of the garage was a door that led into an office. I went inside and glanced around. A man in dark blue pants and matching shirt was sitting at a cheap wooden desk. He looked up at me with droopy eyes.

"Can I help you?" he asked in a Slavic voice.

I walked up to the desk. "Is Davon working today?"

"He's back in the garage."

"May I speak with him for a moment?"

Wariness filled his eyes. "You a friend of his?"

"Something like that."

He frowned. "He's busy right now."

"It'll only take a moment. It's important."

I was tempted to flash my PI badge at him, but I didn't want to get Davon into any trouble, so I resisted. I gave him a hard look, and it worked. He gestured at a door across the room that led to the garage.

"He's working on a Subaru. Make it quick."

I thanked him and hurried through the door before he changed his mind. In the closest bay, an older-model Mazda had the hood up, and a man with dark hair was tinkering on the engine. He glanced up as I walked past him and over to a beat-up Subaru that was on a hydraulic lift. A big man with broad shoulders and long hair pulled into a ponytail was standing underneath the Subaru, his back to me.

"Are you Davon?" I said loudly in order to be heard over the music playing from a radio on a long bench at the back of the garage. Through a window I saw more cars parked in a back lot.

He turned around slowly and I got a better look at him. I'd expected someone younger, maybe because Gabe was only twenty-one, but I placed Davon a bit older, about Sally's age. A scar cut through his left eyebrow, and the sneer on his face made him look sinister. He stared at me with cold black eyes.

"Who wants to know?" he said.

I ignored that. "The man up front said I could talk to you for a few minutes."

He looked over my shoulder, then his eyes settled on me. They hadn't lost any of their chill.

"What do you want?"

"I understand you knew Gabe Culpepper."

He was standing with his feet spread apart, a long screwdriver in his hand. "What's it to you?"

"Did you know he's dead?"

"Get lost." He turned, picked up an impact air wrench from a cart, and held it like a gun, the end pointed at me. He hit the trigger once and a high-pitched whir filled the garage.

I noticed that he didn't seem concerned one way or the other about the news of Gabe's death. I reached into my wallet and showed him my PI badge. It had the effect I'd hoped. Although his eyebrows rose slightly, and his face remained impassive, he was paying attention to me.

"You a cop?" he asked in a low voice.

I shook my head. "A private investigator. Sally Evans hired me."

"Who?" He seemed genuinely puzzled.

"She was dating Gabe." I described her.

Recognition dawned on his face. "Oh, Nightmare Sally. That's what Gabe called her." He studied me. "They think she did it?"

"Did what?" I asked.

"Murdered Gabe."

"Who said anything about murder?"

He glared at me. "Look, man, you come in here flashing that badge, telling me Sally hired you … I can put two and two together."

"She says she's innocent."

"Huh."

I felt motion behind me and I glanced over my shoulder. The man working on the Mazda had moved around the side of the car so he was closer to us. He was doing something in the engine, but it seemed halfhearted, as he was gazing in our direction. Davon gave him a pointed stare and made a show of aiming the impact wrench at him. The man quickly looked the other way.

Davon turned to me. "What do you want from me?"

"Sally said you had a fight with Gabe. She overheard Gabe tell you he didn't want any more of that action."

He swung the wrench back toward me. "So?"

"What did he mean by that?"

"I don't have to talk to you."

He was playing it cool, almost too cool. As if he was nervous, but wasn't going to show it. I suspected he'd had practice with that. He started to turn away.

"That's true, you don't," I said. "But if you're involved in Gabe's murder, I'll dig it up."

He whirled back to me, his demeanor cracked. "I don't know anything!"

"Then talk to me, man. I just want to get to the bottom of this."

Davon took in a deep breath, his nostrils flaring, and I could see him thinking through what he should do. I'm sure he knew that if he didn't talk to me, he'd look suspicious in my eyes. The other man cleared his throat, and Davon glanced at him, then said, "I need a cigarette."

He set the wrench down on the cart with a thud and waved at me to follow him. We walked through a nearby door and stood at the side of the building. Traffic noise from the nearby streets drifted over to us. Davon took a pack of Marlboros from a shirt pocket and lit one up. He gazed at me with narrowed eyes.

"I didn't do anything to Gabe."

"Gabe said something about not wanting that kind of action from you," I repeated. "What does that mean?"

He hesitated. "It was ... some gambling. But I'm not telling you more, okay?"

"All right. Why were you mad at him?"

"We had an argument." He wasn't going to give up information easily.

"About what?"

"Money."

I cocked an eyebrow and waited.

"He owed me some," he said. "But he paid me back," he tacked on quickly, "so it wasn't a big deal."

"Are you saying Sally got it wrong and you weren't mad at Gabe, that you didn't argue with him?"

"Yeah."

"Why did Sally think you were mad at Gabe?"

"Why dontcha ask her?"

"I will," I said.

He was glaring at me defiantly, and I wasn't buying that he was telling me the whole story. But he wasn't going to say more on the subject, either.

"How much money did Gabe owe you?"

"None of your damn business."

I shrugged. "Okay, I'll look into it."

"Yeah, you do that." He stuck the cigarette in the corner of his mouth, crossed his arms, and dared me to press him. I didn't see that going anywhere, and I moved on.

"Did Gabe have a gambling problem?"

"Maybe."

"Where'd he gamble at?"

"Online mostly."

"Anywhere around town?"

He shrugged.

"When's the last time you saw him?" I asked.

"A couple weeks ago, at Club 77."

"Who else was there?"

"Sally."

"She said she hadn't seen you in longer than that."

"She's wrong."

I made a mental note to check with her about that. "And that's when you argued with Gabe?"

"It was after that."

"I thought you said you hadn't argued with Gabe at all."

His eyes narrowed as he realized he'd been caught in a lie. He took the cigarette from his mouth, dropped it on the ground, and crushed it out with his foot. "I gotta go."

"Where were you last Sunday night around eleven?" I said quickly.

"At home."

"Who can verify that?"

"My grandmother. I live with her."

His *grandmother*? Seriously? I almost laughed out loud.

"I told you everything," he snapped. "Now leave me alone."

"Or?"

He stepped close to me and tapped my chest with a finger. "You don't want to know. I got nothin' to say to you, so get lost."

He spun around, opened the door, and disappeared inside. A moment later, I heard the high pitch of the impact wrench. I walked around the side of the building and back through the front entrance. The man in blue was still at the desk.

"You talk to Davon?" he asked.

"Yes." I nodded toward the garage. "What kind of worker is he? Does he show up on time, or give you problems?"

"He's fine." He stared at me, more alert now. "What is going on with him? Why all the questions?"

"Nothing to worry about," I said. "One last thing. What's his last name?"

"Edwards." He held up a finger. "I don't want trouble, okay? You need to talk to Davon again, you talk to him when he gets off work, okay?"

I nodded, thanked him, and walked back outside. As I passed by the garage doors, I glanced toward the Subaru. Davon was standing underneath it, but he was watching me warily. I headed back to my car with one thought rolling around in my head.

Davon was dirty. I wasn't sure what he was hiding, but he hadn't been truthful with me. And I was going to find out why.

CHAPTER THIRTEEN

I got back to the 4-Runner and thought for a moment. Then I pulled out my phone and was about to call Cal when Bogie interrupted me.

"Oh, it's not always easy to know what to do."

It took me a moment to recognize the number. It was Sally.

"Have you found out anything?" she asked the second I answered.

"It's early," I said. "Where are you now?"

"I'm at home, er, Kristen's place. I spent some time with my mother, and I just got here. I don't feel like doing much of anything."

"I'm going to stop by," I said. "We need to talk."

"What's wrong?" She could sense my displeasure.

"I'll tell you when I get there." I wanted to talk to her in person. Much easier to tell when someone's lying.

"Okay," she said. "I'll be here."

I ended the call, started the 4-Runner, and headed to Humboldt Street. On the way to Kristen's apartment, I dialed Cal.

"I've found out something about Gabe," he said without a greeting.

"Oh yeah?"

"He was arrested for assault two years ago."

"That fits with what Spillman told me."

"Uh-huh. Did she tell you that Gabe's a high-school dropout, he doesn't have much money, that he has a checkered employment record?"

I laughed. "We didn't get that far."

"This guy sounds like a real piece of work."

"True. Did you see any indication that he was an online gambler?"

"No. He's only got two credit cards and I didn't see any charges like that, or any from his bank account, either."

"It appears I was lied to."

"What?"

"Never mind. I need your special skills again," I said. "Do you have time?"

"Sure."

"First, can you look up a man named Davon Edwards? I want everything you can find on him."

"Check his background and financials, that kind of thing?"

"Yeah, and I want to know if he's been in any kind of trouble with the law, or if he's registered any guns."

"That goes without saying."

"Good."

"What about Sally Evans? You want me to do the same for her?" he asked.

"Spillman confirmed Sally was arrested for public indecency."

"You think she told you everything? After all, Sally's her prime suspect."

"Spillman's never lied to me before," I mused, "but she is directly involved in the investigation, so she might've held something back." I was reluctant to think she would do that. "And I *know* Sally has lied to me."

"Oh really? I'll check her, too." I heard typing. "I need a little time for this. I'll call you later tonight."

"That'll work, thanks," I said. "Oh, since you're checking on Sally, find out if she's been licensed to carry a gun, or if she registered a gun."

"Will do."

And then he was gone. I cranked a Smiths greatest hits CD and drove south on Downing. Ten minutes later, I parked on Humboldt Street. Kristen lived in a basement apartment in a brown-brick building on the corner of Humboldt and Thirteenth. I walked down five steps to her door. Through an open window, I heard a woman singing to the soft strumming of an acoustic guitar. Sally, I assumed. I stood on a tiny landing and listened. Her voice was low and sultry, and the song was slow. Definitely not the hard beat of the techno music Gabe had favored. I tapped on the door and the music stopped. A moment later, Sally opened the door.

"Hey," she said. "Come on in." She gestured at a long couch.

I stepped into a small living room dominated by a large TV. An acoustic guitar lay in an open case between the couch and an empty bookcase. A doorway led to a kitchen that barely had enough room for a refrigerator and stove. And dishes were piled high in the sink.

"Have a seat." She quickly pushed folded sheets, a blanket, and a notebook onto the arm of the couch. Then she sat down. I remained standing and glanced around.

"Is Kristen here?" I asked.

She shook her head and stared at me nervously as she wrapped her hair around her fingers. "What's going on?"

"Why didn't you tell me you'd been going to the gun range with Kristen?"

Her jaw dropped, and then she shrugged. "I ... uh, I didn't think it was important."

"Did you tell the police that you'd been going to the gun range?"

"Of course not."

"Why not?"

"Because I ..." Her voice trailed off. "They didn't need to know."

"They'll find out."

"So?"

"It makes you look guilty," I said.

She tipped her chin up defiantly. "Why? Lots of people go to gun ranges."

"Really?" I threw up my hands. "You can't figure it out? It makes it look like you were learning how to shoot a gun so you could murder your boyfriend."

She gasped. "It was just for fun!"

I took a second to muster up some patience. "You are the most likely suspect in Gabe's murder, and the police are looking for a motive to pin it on you. If you want me to help you, you can't hold anything back."

"I'm not. I just didn't think anything of it."

I crossed my arms and stared at her. "Is there anything else you want to tell me?"

"No," she said. "But if I think of something, I'll let you know."

"Do you own a gun?"

"I told you no."

I tipped my head at her. "You've already lied to me."

"I don't own a gun." She emphasized each word carefully.

"Have you ever owned one?"

"No."

"I'm having someone check that," I said. "If they find out otherwise, or if I find out you've lied about *anything*, I'll drop the case."

Her lower lip quivered. "I'm telling you the truth."

I let her sit uncomfortably for a moment. She kept playing with her hair, but now she was biting her lower lip, too.

"I talked to Davon," I finally said.

"You found him?"

I nodded. "He says he saw you and Gabe two weeks ago at Club 77."

"So?"

"You said you hadn't seen Davon in a couple of months."

Her cheeks flushed red. "I guess I was wrong."

"So Davon is right."

She shrugged. "I guess."

I drew in a breath and let it out very slowly. She was trying my patience. "Sally, you need to do me a favor."

"What?"

"You need to start focusing a little more, or you're going to find yourself in prison for murder."

She glanced away. When she looked back, there were tears in her eyes. Lord help me, I'm a sucker for a damsel in distress, and this was no exception.

"I'm sorry I'm being so flaky," she whispered.

"Don't worry about it," I said in a soothing tone. Then I moved on. "Davon said that Gabe was a gambler, mostly online."

"That's news to me."

"You never saw him gambling?"

"No. I even remember his next-door neighbor inviting him to a poker night, and Gabe said no, that he hated poker."

"It appears Davon lied to me," I said.

"All I know is if Gabe gambled, it was never around me."

I thought for a second. "Does your supervisor at work know what's going on?"

She shook her head. "I called in sick today, but I'll go in tomorrow."

"If Gabe's murder is in the news, they'll find out. You might want to talk to your boss about what's going on."

"Are you still going to talk to him?"

"If he'll see me."

"He might fire me." She let out a huge sigh.

I nodded, then pointed at the notebook sitting on top of the sheets and blanket. "Were you working on a song before I got here?"

"Yeah. It's not much."

"May I see it?"

"Yeah." She handed the notebook to me.

I read the lyrics on the page. The song was about being in a bad relationship and feeling trapped. I had to admit, it had a haunting quality to it.

"This is good," I said.

"Thanks."

I noticed that other pages were filled with writing. I held up the notebook. "Is this an older notebook?"

"Yeah, one that Gabe gave back to me. You can look through it."

I flipped through a few pages and read them. Some pages contained songs, some seemed more of a rap rhyme, and some were comedic vignettes or jokes. I didn't get the humor in a lot of them, but a few were pretty funny. I chuckled.

"What?" she said.

I handed the notebook back to her. "Kristen said you were funny, and that maybe you missed your calling."

She shrugged. "Maybe." She sighed again. "What're you going to do now?"

"You really did see a man on the fire escape outside Gabe's apartment?"

"Yes! I'm not lying."

"The police didn't find anyone in the building who saw a man leaving through the alley." I held up a hand to stop her protests. "I'm going by Gabe's place to see if I can find anyone who *did* see someone, but didn't want to tell the police."

"Oh, I hope you do."

"It might not lead anywhere."

"But it might." She was grasping at anything that would give her hope.

I went to the door and opened it. "I'll be in touch soon. If you think of anything you forgot, call me, all right? We're on the same team."

She nodded. I let myself out, and before I'd reached the sidewalk, I heard her voice without the guitar, this time singing the song she'd been working on when I'd arrived. Her voice wasn't the greatest, but the lyrics were good, ones that could get under your skin. I listened for a minute longer, and the line "or I'll end up in jail" drifted out the window. It sent chills through me.

CHAPTER FOURTEEN

In five minutes, I drove back to Gabe's apartment on Race Street. It was almost four, and parking spots on the street were filling up. I had to park down the block and walk back to the entrance. I went inside and scanned the mailboxes. Apartment 303 was labeled "Hernandez." I pushed the small call button beneath the name. After no one answered on the speaker, I punched a bunch of other call buttons and waited again. A moment later, the door buzzed. Someone either was waiting for a visitor, or they didn't get the idea behind having a security door to keep out strangers.

I climbed the stairs to the third floor and walked down the hall. Apartment 302 had yellow crime scene ribbon tacked across the door. I couldn't resist checking the doorknob. It was locked. I went to 303 and knocked. No one came to the door, and I knocked again with the same result. I frowned and turned away. I'd try Hernandez again later.

With that thought in mind, I went to the other end of the hall and knocked on the door, but no one was home. I sighed and moved on to the other apartments on the third floor. In one, a woman was home, but she said she hadn't been home the night when Gabe had been killed, and she didn't know him.

I trudged down to the second floor, started at one end of the hall, and knocked on doors. One young woman barely let me ask about Gabe before she shut the door in my face, but then I hit paydirt in apartment 202. A man with a young face but with gray around his temples answered. I explained who I was and asked him if he'd heard about Gabe Culpepper's murder.

"That guy upstairs? Yeah, I heard about it. I didn't know him."

"Were you home that night?"

He glanced into the hall. "You a cop?"

"No." I pulled out my PI license and showed him.

He studied it closely, then stood in the doorway and waited for me to say more. I continued before he changed his mind about me.

"Were you home that night?" I repeated as I put my wallet away.

"Uh-huh."

"Did you hear a gunshot?"

He hesitated. "I had the TV on and I didn't hear anything."

I could tell he was holding something back. "But what?"

He shifted from foot to foot. "I saw a guy outside my window, going down the fire escape. I swear it was a ghost because the guy's face was white as a sheet. Scared me to death. I'm not afraid to admit that it took me a second to go and look, but by then, whoever was there was gone."

"You said it was a man?"

He shrugged. "I think so. I didn't get a good look and it could've been a woman."

"Was he in a hoodie?"

"Yeah."

"Did you call the police?"

He snorted. "What would they do, other than think I was crazy?"

"Did you talk to the police about Gabe's death?"

"Yeah, but I didn't tell them about that guy."

"Why not?"

He shrugged. "I don't want to get involved."

"I see. Did you know Gabe?"

"No. I saw him around a time or two, but I didn't even know his name until some people in the building told me about his murder."

"Anything else you can tell me?"

"No."

I thanked him for his time, then tried the rest of the apartments, but the tenants who I talked to hadn't heard anything of note, nor had they seen any ghost-like person outside the building the night Gabe had been murdered.

I returned to the third floor, and when I reached the landing, a young Hispanic man was walking past Gabe's apartment. He was small, probably no more than five-six, with short, black hair that was slicked back. I paused on the landing and watched him stop at 303.

"Excuse me?" I said as I headed toward him.

He stopped, his key in his hand, and gazed at me cautiously. "Yeah?"

"Are you Luis?"

"Who wants to know?"

I gestured at Gabe's apartment. "You heard about Gabe?"

"Who hasn't?" The wariness remained.

"Sally Evans said you're friends with Gabe."

"Nightmare Sally?"

I was beginning to loathe that nickname, and agreed with Kristen Dalrymple, who said it had been mean of Gabe to call her that.

"Yes," I said. "She said I should talk to you." I was again shading the truth.

"Is she in trouble?" He unlocked the door and opened it.

"She's a suspect in Gabe's murder."

He swore. "Sally? No way."

I glanced up and down the hallway. "Mind if we talk inside?"

"You a cop?"

I shook my head. "I'm private."

He stared at me for a moment. "You don't think she did it." It was a statement, and within the tone was his feeling as well.

"That's what I'm trying to find out."

Two women came out a door at the other end of the hall. They were giggling as they walked toward the stairs, but they had their eyes on us. They lingered on the landing, watching us. I pointed behind Luis, into his apartment.

"Could we talk inside?" I repeated, then gave a slight nod of my head toward the women. "Unless you want everyone to hear our conversation."

He gave a halfhearted wave at the women, then said to me, "Uh, sure."

I followed him into an apartment that had the same layout as Gabe's. But where Gabe had cheap furniture, Luis seemed to be trying for a modern vibe à la IKEA. He gestured for me to sit on a small white couch while he went into the kitchen and returned with a beer. He didn't offer me one.

He leaned against a large desk that had a substantial monitor on it. A laptop sat nearby, and I also spotted a tablet on a coffee table.

"So what do you want?" he asked.

I got right to the point. "Any idea who might've killed Gabe?"

He shrugged. "It doesn't make sense, you ask me. Gabe was an okay dude, at least with me."

"From what I can gather, he was arrogant and people didn't like him."

He snorted. "They're just jealous."

"Of what?"

"Gabe was a cool deejay."

"You saw him at some clubs?"

He nodded and took a swig of his beer. "Mostly at Club 77. He had all the girls wanting him. And he mixes his own stuff, too. Mostly techno."

"I've heard he was producing some songs."

"And some were good. He was going places."

"How do you know?"

"I heard it, man, all the videos and stuff. He told me he was working on a big deal, that it was the break he was waiting for."

"Hmm," I said. "How do you know that wasn't just Gabe talking big?"

He brushed that aside. "Nah, man, he was onto something."

"But you don't know what."

"Well, I dunno ..." He didn't finish the sentence.

"What?"

"Nothing. He's just got it going, trust me."

"Did Gabe have a job?"

"I don't think so. Nothing regular anyway."

"Where'd he get money?"

"I think he had something going on with this big dude I saw

around."

I described Davon.

"Yeah, that's him," Luis said. "I saw him one time out in the hall, arguing with Gabe about selling some stuff. I don't know what it was about, but that big dude was maaaad at Gabe."

"Did he threaten Gabe?"

"Like he was going to do something to him?"

I nodded.

He thought about that as he fiddled with a button on his shirt. "He said something like Gabe better not tell anyone. Something like that. I just know that dude wasn't happy."

"Was anyone else mad at Gabe?"

"I don't know."

"Were you here the night Gabe was murdered?"

"No, I was out with some friends."

"Sally says she saw someone on the fire escape outside Gabe's window. Have you heard anyone in the building talking about that?"

He shook his head.

"Did Gabe ever gamble?"

"I don't think so. I even asked him to come with me to a poker night with my buddies, but he said he hated poker and didn't really gamble."

"Huh." I wondered if Gabe hadn't been straight with Luis, or, as I'd thought before, had Davon lied to me. Since Sally hadn't been aware of Gabe gambling either, my bet – no pun intended – was on Davon lying.

Luis interrupted my thoughts. "Gabe was into music, man. We even put some stuff together. Let me show you."

He set down his beer and grabbed the tablet off the table before I could protest, swiped at the screen, and began tapping it. "Here's something we did a while back."

The video showed Luis and Gabe at their computers, or dancing in front of a building, as they rapped a song. The video, and the song, seemed amateur to me. But then, it also wasn't the kind of music I liked, so what kind of critic was I?

"It's good," I said politely.

"Yeah, Gabe did some better stuff."

He tapped the screen again, found Gabe's Facebook page, and showed me a video post. This one was flashier, with a techno sound and lots of graphics.

"Gabe did this?" I asked.

He nodded. "He's good, huh."

"Yes."

I noticed another post that Gabe had shared, of a man in a black-and-white mask standing near a building with a skateboard.

"Is that Gabe?"

"Nah, that's Masta Dig. Don't you know him?"

"Vaguely," I murmured, thinking about my conversation with the Goofballs.

"This dude is awesome!"

He pressed "play" and the video began.

"Masta Dig comes to you again with a great trick," a disembodied voice said. "Check it out." The man put his skateboard down, then skated across the sidewalk while he rapped some lyrics that I couldn't understand. Luis danced to the rhythm. Then Masta Dig crashed into a tree. The masked man raised his arms and yelled, "Masta Dig can do anything!" The video ended.

Luis busted out laughing. "He's hilarious."

"I'll take your word for it," I said. "Who's the man behind the mask?"

"Uh, nobody knows. That's what makes it fun. Sometimes he dares people to find out who he is by telling them a bit about where he films the videos, but no one's figured it out. And look." He pointed at the screen. "He's got over five million followers, and he's getting more every day. Man, I wish I had that."

"You do this kind of thing?"

"Nah, man, I just meant I wish I had that kind of talent."

If you could call what Masta Dig was doing "talent," I thought. "Huh," was all I managed to say.

"That dude's gotta be raking in the dough. Or if he isn't, he soon will be."

"How so?"

"Advertising, man." He poked a finger at the screen again. "He's getting YouTube ads, and then some of these guys, like Logan Paul and King Bach, actually have companies paying them to promote their products."

"Who?"

"Logan Paul and King Bach. They're hilarious, too. They've even got movie parts and stuff like that. Think about it. Hollywood, man."

"I had no idea these social media personalities were that big."

"They are," he said with awe in his voice. "And Masta Dig is putting up new videos all the time, and they crack me up."

I was getting an education, but it wasn't getting me any closer to finding Gabe's killer. I handed the tablet back to him.

"I really appreciate your help."

"No problem, man. I hope you find Gabe's killer."

I pulled out a business card. "If you think of anything about Gabe that might be important, give me a call."

"What would I think of?"

I shrugged. "I'm not sure."

"Uh, okay."

Lord, I felt like I was talking to one of the Goofballs.

"Thanks," I said.

When I left, Luis was back on the tablet. By his laughing, I assumed he was watching another Masta Dig video. I didn't get it.

CHAPTER FIFTEEN

When I got back to the 4-Runner, I googled "Davon Edwards" and found what appeared to be a current address near Fortieth and Colorado Boulevard. I poked around a few White Pages sites, but I couldn't access any listings of Davon's relatives, so I googled the address. It took a bit more searching, but I found a site that listed a Francine Johnson at that address. I googled her name, and found that she was born in 1945.

"That'd be about the right date of birth for her to be Davon's grandmother," I said to no one. "Let's see if my assumption is correct."

I put my phone away and headed to Francine Johnson's house.

» » » » »

Francine Johnson lived in a small house on Jackson Street that had a tiny brown yard that was crying for attention. I pushed through an old picket-fence gate that badly needed paint and up the sidewalk to a front entrance with a rickety screen door. I rang the bell and waited. A moment later, it was opened by a buxom woman in a threadbare yellow bathrobe and dirty white slippers, with curlers in her gray hair. She held the collar of a German Shepherd as she peered at me though the screen door. The sound of a game show and the smell of coffee drifted out to me.

"Yes?" Her voice was squeaky and small, like a mouse.

"Are you Francine Johnson?" I asked.

"I am." She pulled her robe tight around her chest.

"I'd like to talk to you about your grandson, Davon." Before I had a chance to show her my ID, or say anything more, she interrupted me.

"What's that boy gotten himself into?"

"I'm not sure he's gotten into anything," I began.

"Well, if you expect me to bail him out of jail again, I'm not going to do it. He's not getting any cash from me." She emphasized this with a sweeping motion of a wrinkly hand. "And you tell him that he made his choice leaving here, so he can't come back. You got that?"

"He doesn't live here now?"

Her eyes narrowed and her lips went in and out as she stared at me. "That's what I just said."

"Was he here on Sunday night?"

"That boy hasn't been around for weeks. I don't know what he's up to these days, and I don't want to know."

"Hmm," I said. Since she was talking, I needed to get as much information from her as I could. "I must have misunderstood him."

"You must have," she said matter-of-factly.

"Where does he live now?"

She let go of the dog's collar and he sat down, but he looked up and emitted a low growl. "How should I know? That boy doesn't tell me anything." She narrowed her eyes. "But he did try to call me a little bit ago."

"What did he want?"

She waved a hand around. "I don't want to get involved in whatever tomfoolery he's gotten himself into, and I didn't answer. He didn't leave a message, either."

Maybe calling to tell her to cover for his alibi, I thought.

"Where did you see him? Jail?" She didn't seem concerned, but curious.

"He's working at CJ's Auto Repair," I said.

"For how long?"

"I don't know." Somehow she'd turned the tables and was interrogating me. "What did Davon do before that job?" I asked, taking control of the conversation again.

Her lips were working again as she mused, almost unaware of my presence. "I'm surprised he has a job at all. That boy is trouble, through and through. I hate to say it about my own flesh and blood, but it's the truth. Though, Lord, I tried with him. But he was so angry, his momma had a drinking problem and couldn't raise him." She shook her head sadly. "I don't know what I did with that one, either. I blame myself. I married a good-for-nothing alcoholic, and she took after him. Got herself pregnant too young, and the daddy didn't stick around. She couldn't take care of Davon, and I took him in."

"What kind of trouble was Davon in?"

"Drinking. Drugs. Stealing. I don't know what else. That boy and his friends were bad news. They didn't want to go to school. I tried to get Davon to go, but he dropped out and ended up in jail for stealing a car." She let out a bitter laugh. "Isn't that funny, him working at a car repair place. He was good with cars, though, had a mind for that."

"Maybe he's turning over a new leaf," I said.

"Huh, wouldn't that be nice." She poked at her curlers. "Someone might've got through to him."

"Did Davon own any guns?"

"I saw one in his bedroom once. I told him to get rid of it. I didn't want them in the house."

"Did he get rid of it?"

"I never saw any around again."

That wasn't much of an answer, but I let it go.

"Did Davon ever mention a man named Gabe Culpepper?" I asked.

She shook her head. "Never heard of him."

I described Gabe.

"No," she said. "Doesn't ring a bell, but I didn't like Davon having his friends over. They're disrespectful, and I wouldn't put it past them to steal from me. And they were noisy, didn't care if they were bothering me. They'd go in Davon's room and play their music loud. That's what Davon and his friends were into, cars, music, partying, and his dirty pictures."

"Huh." I cleared my throat.

"Yep. He thought I didn't know about that, his finding the nudie stuff on the Internet. But I did. Disgusting."

"So if Davon didn't have a job, how did he get money?" I asked.

"He didn't get it from me." She sniffed. "He probably stole stuff. Or sold drugs. But that boy, I'll tell you, he lives in a dream world. Doesn't think he has to earn anything, he'll just strike it rich somehow. But that's not the way it works, now is it?"

I thought it was a rhetorical question and I waited for her to go on, but she glared at me, and I murmured, "No, it is not."

"You got to work hard. Look at me. Forty years I worked in a school cafeteria. I didn't make much money, but I've managed to pay off this house. It's not much, but I've got some money in the bank, and I'll be all right in my old age. Not that Davon, or my daughter, would care."

"Good for you," I said, then focused her back on her grandson. "Did Davon ever gamble?"

She pursed her lips. "Not that I know of, but then again, it wouldn't surprise me. I just don't understand that boy, and why he would want to cause me so much trouble. Do you know what it's like to worry like I have? My blood pressure is sky high. I don't know how I haven't had a heart attack."

It seemed I'd gotten as much information as I could. I quickly thanked her and got out of there before I heard more about her woes. As I walked back to my car, I thought about Davon. One thing was clear: he had lied about his alibi for the night Gabe Culpepper had been killed. Why? Because he'd murdered Gabe? I didn't know, but I was going to find out.

CHAPTER SIXTEEN

It was now after five, and when I got in the 4-Runner, I googled CJ's Auto Repair again. It closed at six. Perfect. I'd go by there again, but this time I wasn't going to attempt to talk to Davon, in part because he'd made it clear that he wouldn't speak to me, and I didn't expect that to change. However, I was going to follow him and see where that led me.

Even though it was rush hour, traffic wasn't too bad as I made my way on less busy streets back to the repair shop. I arrived with half an hour to spare. I parked partway down Marion Street, where I could look across a small triangular lot and see the front of the shop.

I pulled out my binoculars and surreptitiously watched for Davon. A few cars drove past on Thirty-sixth, but no one noticed me. A little after six, Davon emerged with the other man I'd seen in the garage. They walked to a small lot near the shop and I lost sight of them. A moment later, an older-model brown Trans Am pulled out of the lot. Davon was at the wheel.

He drove north on Lawrence Street, and I left some distance between us before I fell in behind him. He meandered north and then east, onto Fortieth, then to Clayton, and I had a good guess where he was going. The Rat Tavern. Sure enough, he parked near the bar and went inside. I found a parking place down the block where I could see the Trans Am, and was watching the bar when I suddenly realized I hadn't talked to Willie to let her know I wouldn't be home anytime soon. I pulled out my phone and called her.

"Hey, where are you?" she answered. "I was wondering about dinner."

"The day's gotten away from me," I said. "And I don't think I'll be home anytime soon."

She sighed. "I wish you would've called."

"Sorry. I'll make it up to you."

"You better." She laughed. "What's going on?"

I filled her in on my day, and ended with, "I'm going to follow Davon and see where it leads me. He's up to something, I'm just not sure what."

"Okay, be careful."

"Always."

I ended the call, then googled the Rat's phone number and dialed it.

"Rat Tavern," Ella's sultry voice could barely be heard over the music in the background.

"Ella, it's Reed."

"Oh, sure, honey. Did you find Sally?"

I hesitated. "I did." I didn't want to tell her about Sally's predicament right now. "She's doing okay."

"Oh, that's good. I don't know about that girl sometimes. You tell her I said hello."

"Will do."

"Anyway, what can I do for you?"

"I'm following a man named Davon Edwards." I described him. "You may have seen him with Gabe."

"Yeah, I know who you mean. He's here."

"What's he doing?"

The sound of the music faded into a dull thump, replaced by the clinking of dishes. She'd moved into the kitchen.

"He's drinking with another fella, and they ordered dinner."

"Do you know the other man?"

"I've seen him around a time or two with Davon, but I don't know his name."

"What does this man look like?"

"He's kind of stocky, with a shaved head, earrings, and he's got tattoos, but only on his left arm." It was a good description. "What's going on? Does this have to do with Sally?"

"I'm not sure," I said truthfully.

"Well, I hope you figure out whatever you're trying to figure out," she said.

"Thanks."

I put my phone away and watched the bar. Minutes turned into an hour, and then some. My stomach growled, and I wished I was having dinner with Willie instead of sitting in my car waiting for Davon. I wondered if Bogie ever got tired of stakeouts. The sky morphed into a dark blue and the light faded. And then Davon walked out of the Rat with the man Ella had described. I watched them through the binoculars.

The bald man's pate glinted in the moonlight as he talked and smoked with Davon in front of the bar. Then the man threw his head back and laughed, clapped Davon on the shoulder, then turned and went back in the bar. Davon tossed his cigarette into the street and walked to the Trans Am. He got in and fired up the engine, creating a racket in the street. Then it peeled away from the curb. I waited a bit and followed.

Davon went south to Fortieth and then east. He was right near his grandmother's house, and I'd no sooner wondered if he would stop by to see her than he turned onto Jackson.

"You need her help with your alibi," I said aloud, "but it's too late."

I drove slowly past Jackson and saw the Trans Am partway down the street. Davon was just getting out. I parked on Thirty-seventh, noticed an alley, and ran down it. When I reached the back of Francine Johnson's house, I paused to catch my breath and listen. It was almost dark, and the alley was in deep shadows.

I stepped up to a dilapidated one-car garage that faced the alley and peered around the corner. A chain-link fence surrounded a small backyard, but I couldn't tell if Francine's German Shepherd was outside. I reached out and gave the fence a quick shake. A few houses away, a dog barked, but no sound came from Francine's yard. Good, no four-legged friend to announce my presence – or attack me. I let myself into the yard and stole up to the back of the house. A kitchen window was open and I heard voices coming from inside.

"… can speak to who I want to," Francine was saying, her voice annoyingly squeaky.

"What'd you say to him?" Davon's voice was low and threatening.

"I told him that you've been nothing but trouble," she said, and started into a tirade.

"Shut up!" he snapped.

I cringed. I would never have talked to my grandparents that way.

Francine made a peep, and he snapped at her again.

"Listen," he snarled. "If that guy, or anyone else, comes here and asks where I was on Sunday night, you tell them I was here. Got it?"

"I will do no such thing. You weren't here."

"I'm warning you," he said.

"What have you gotten yourself into?"

"None of your business. Just do what I tell you, all right?"

I heard footsteps, and then a door slammed. I hurried to the corner of the house and peeked around. A moment later, Davon walked down the sidewalk and disappeared. Then I became aware of Francine's voice.

"Do you want to go outside?"

She's letting the dog out! I thought.

I dashed across the yard and raced through the gate just as I heard the back door open. Francine may not have heard me, but the dog did. He peeled across the yard, barking ferociously. Francine called out to him, but I didn't hear what she said because I was running as fast as I could down the alley. I reached the 4-Runner, hopped in and was about to start it when the Trans Am flew past me. It turned south on Colorado Boulevard and I followed, tailing Davon to a Burger King, where he went to the drive-through window and ordered something. Then he went south again. Twenty minutes later, he parked outside a small three-story apartment building near Swedish Hospital. He carried his meal as he climbed a set of stairs to the second floor and disappeared inside a unit. Seconds later, a window by the door lit up. I parked on the street and waited. Fifteen minutes later, my phone rang and I jumped, then quickly answered it.

"Hey, Cal."

"O Great Detective. Do you have time for what I learned on Davon Edwards?"

I stared up at Davon's apartment. Nothing had changed.

"I'm just sitting here," I said.

"It's not pretty. He's got a juvenile record – don't ask me how I got that – for shoplifting and drug possession, and he graduated from that to being charged as an adult for auto theft, and drug possession again. He's never registered a gun, but that doesn't mean that he couldn't have stolen one."

"Right," I agreed.

"He's spent a couple years in prison," Cal went on, "and he was on parole for almost a year. He was a high school dropout, but got his GED in prison. He has a little money in a checking account, and the last known address I can find for him is on Jackson Street."

"That's his grandmother's house, and he's not living there now."

"Huh. He must not have things like an electric bill in his name."

"Hold on," I said. "I can get you an address now."

"You're with him?" He was surprised.

"Watching his place. Or the place he went into. Let me call you back."

"Sure thing."

And he was gone.

I could see an address for Davon's building, but not a unit number, so I ran across the street and up to the apartment on the end. Once I figured out how the units were numbered, it was easy to figure out Davon's. I ran back to the 4-Runner, got in, and called Cal back.

I rattled off the street address, then said, "Davon's in 203."

He did a quick search. "A man named Gregory Reichs lives there." He spelled the last name.

"Never heard of him," I said.

"Maybe he has nothing to do with your case."

I stared at Davon's door. "Could be."

"While you try and piece that together, let me tell you what else I found out."

"About what?" My mind was drawing a blank on what I'd asked him to do.

"I looked up Sally Evans."

"Oh, right."

"Spillman didn't lie to you," he said. "Sally was only arrested for public indecency. Other than that, she's clean."

"Good to know. What about Sally owning a gun?"

"I can't find that she ever owned a gun. Did she lie to you about that?"

"Apparently not."

"That's good, right?" he said with a hint of sarcasm in his voice.

"Yes."

"You need anything else?"

"No, thanks for the help."

"What's your next move?"

"I think I'm wasting my time here." I sighed. "I'm going home. I'll pick things up tomorrow."

"Sounds like a good plan. Oh, would you mind if I stopped by tomorrow?"

"Not at all, but what brings you into town?"

"I've got a morning meeting with a client, and then another afternoon meeting. I tried to schedule them back-to-back, but that didn't work and I'll have time to kill between appointments. I thought I could work at your place instead of making two trips into town."

"Sure. I won't be around, and I'll check with Willie, but I doubt she'll mind."

"Thanks. My meeting's at eight, so sometime after that."

"No problem."

I ended the call, put my phone back in my pocket, and stared at Davon's apartment. It appeared he was in for the night. I frowned, started up my car, and left. I now knew where he lived, and that he had lied about his alibi for the night Gabe Culpepper had been killed. But why? The obvious reason was that Davon was guilty of murder. But I'd have to prove that.

CHAPTER SEVENTEEN

I'd covered a lot of ground in one day, and as I drove home, my mind was racing with what to do next. I assumed Davon would be at work the next day, but what would he do after that? I had no idea, but I intended to watch him and find out. In the meantime, I needed to see if I could find the mysterious man who'd argued with Gabe the night he'd been murdered. Sally had said that man seemed to know the owner of Club 77, and if I could track down said bar owner, he might be able to tell me who that man was. I was still mulling over my plans when my phone rang.

"Hello?"

"Reed, it's Sally. I was just wondering how things went today."

"I'm still running down some leads," I said, not ready to tell her everything. I still wasn't completely sure I trusted her.

"If you go by my work, I won't be there. I told them I needed a leave of absence, but I didn't say why. They might know about Gabe, but I was too embarrassed to ask."

"What're you going to do in the meantime?"

She hesitated. "Hang around here, I guess. Maybe visit my mother."

"Those are good ideas. It's possible the police are following you, and you don't want your activities to make them even more suspicious of you."

"They would follow me?"

"It's possible," I repeated.

"Oh," she said slowly. "This is bad."

"Yes, it is. I'll call you when I have an update."

"Okay, thanks."

I ended the call, and as I drove up Broadway, I listened to music and continued to ponder my investigation. When I got home, I ran into the Goofballs, who were just coming home.

"Hey, Reed," they said in unison.

"Hi guys," I said with smile. "Were you playing pool tonight?"

"Uh-huh," Ace said.

"If you're up for it, I could use your help," I said.

On the way home, I had wondered if Sally was really planning to lay low, but I couldn't babysit her all day. However, I'd formed a plan, and the Goofballs were part of it – if they would agree to help. "I need you to watch someone for me, if you have time."

"Who?" This from Ace.

"There's a woman named Sally I want you to keep an eye on tomorrow."

Ace lowered his voice conspiratorially. "Why? Is she a suspect in a murder or something?"

"Let's just say I want to make sure she's not lying to me about what she's doing," I said. "The problem is, I have some other people I need to talk to, and I can't spend my whole day watching her. Do you have to work?"

"I'm off this week," Deuce said.

"And I don't work tomorrow," Ace chimed in, "so this is perfect."

"I don't know," Deuce said. "Just sitting around watching someone can be boring."

"But," Ace held up a hand. "What if she leaves, can we follow her?"

"Yes, you can," I said.

"Really?" they both said at once.

I'd surprised them, since I normally didn't want them to do anything that could put them in harm's way, such as following someone. And even though the art of surveillance could be very tricky, since Sally Evans was a ditz, I didn't think she'd even notice them following her, and the Goofballs would likely not be put in any precarious situations.

"If you have to follow her, you'll need to be careful," I said, then discussed what they should do. I gave them her address, told them what car she drove, and described what she looked like. "Why don't you split up the time into shifts? Ace, you could watch her place for a couple hours, then switch with Deuce. While you watch her apartment, don't draw attention to yourselves, okay? Move your car to different places on the street, and maybe get out and walk around. If she leaves and you follow her, call me."

"Right." Ace saluted.

"This'll be fun," Deuce said.

I hoped they would still think that after they'd spent a few hours watching Sally's apartment.

"Keep in mind, she may not go anywhere," I said, trying to temper their expectations.

They nodded, but I could tell they didn't really believe me. I thanked them, waved goodbye, and went up the stairs on the side of the building. When I let myself into my condo, Willie was sitting on the couch. The late news was on the TV, but she was paying attention to the kitten.

"Hey, hon, how'd the rest of your evening go?" she asked as she scratched the kitten's head.

I went over and gave her a kiss. "Not bad."

"Did you catch the bad guy?"

"Nope." I was so tired, my mind was a blank. Was it just today that I'd spoken with Brenda and Sally at the Starbucks?

"You missed dinner for nothing?" She grinned. "Just kidding."

I reached down and petted the kitten. "How's he doing?"

"The vet says he's fine, he just needs to put on a little weight. I bought some food for him, and some toys."

"So he's staying?"

She held him up to me. "Isn't he just adorable? You wouldn't throw this little guy out, would you?"

I pursed my lips and stared at the kitten. He *was* cute. "I'm being ganged up on," I said with a grin.

She changed the subject. "You want to watch a movie?"

"You don't have to work early?"

"Yeah, but I miss you, so I'll stay up for a while."

"Then a movie it is, but I'm starving. Let me fix a sandwich and you pick out something." I snapped my fingers. "Oh, before I forget, Cal wants to stop by tomorrow." I explained his plans.

"That's not a problem. Tell him to make himself at home."

I loved that Willie got along with my best friend. "I love you," I said.

She tipped her head to the side. "I love you, too."

I leaned down and kissed her again, and she put a hand on the back of my neck. The kiss was long and lingering. When we came up for air, I took her hand and led her to the bedroom. I never fixed my sandwich, but I didn't care.

»»»»»

The next morning, Willie left early and I dawdled over breakfast, then I checked on the Goofball Brothers. Ace had taken the first shift this morning as I'd suggested. He said that Sally's white Hyundai was parked near her building, and that he'd even seen her come out and talk to a neighbor for a bit and then go back into her apartment.

"Okay, call me if you see her go anywhere," I said.

I ended the call, showered, dressed, and went into my office. It's my sanctuary, the one place that I have not allowed Willie to redecorate. It has my favorite things in it, including rare framed posters of *The Big Sleep* and *The Maltese Falcon*, both with Bogie, and *The Postman Always Rings Twice*, with Lana Turner and John Garfield. This last one is my most treasured possession because Willie gave it to me as a wedding gift. It showed how much she really knew me.

I sat down at my desk and logged onto the computer. While it booted up, I glanced at the books on the floor-to-ceiling shelves that are filled with first editions and thought I was forgetting something. Then the doorbell rang.

"Oh, yeah," I said to myself as I got up. "Cal's coming over."

I went to the front door and opened it. "Good morning."

"If you call fighting rush-hour traffic to a meeting good," he said as he stepped past me and into the living room. He had a crazy look in his brown eyes as he ran a hand over his wavy hair.

"Be glad you don't have to fight traffic every day," I said.

"I am. Thanks for letting me hang out here."

"No problem."

The kitten ran up and started climbing up his pant leg. "Hey!" He took a step back, the kitten clinging to his leg. "What's this? Ow!"

"A kitten," I said drily.

"I *know* that. What's it doing here?"

He very carefully pulled it off his leg and set it down. The kitten, undeterred, swiped at Cal's hand. I grabbed the kitten before he could scratch Cal.

"I think we're going to adopt it," I said.

Cal stared at me. "It's going to be around here? Now?"

I patted his shoulder. "You'll survive."

"Does it have a name?"

"It's a he, and we haven't named him yet." I changed the subject. "How'd your meeting go?"

"Fine, although they were upset that their systems aren't as secure as they thought."

I eyed his blue slacks and white shirt. "And you have another meeting this afternoon?"

"Uh-huh. A potential new client."

"Make sure you get the cat hair off your clothes."

He looked at his slacks. "Oh, man!"

"You'll survive," I said again.

He sighed dramatically and held up his backpack. "Where can I work?"

"In my office," I said and started down the hall. "Unless you prefer the kitchen."

"Your office is fine."

"Help yourself to anything in the fridge."

"Will do."

He followed me into my office.

"I need to do a few things, and then I'll be leaving," I said.

He nodded as he put his backpack down and pulled out his laptop. "No problem." He put the laptop on the corner of the desk, opened it up, and turned it on. "Anything I can help you with?"

"I'm looking up Club 77," I said as I began typing. The kitten leaped up into my lap and started purring. "Hey, little guy. Whatcha doin'?"

I petted him for a moment and Cal rolled his eyes at me.

I ignored him and continued. "I need to find the owner. Sally said his name is Rick, but she didn't have a last name." I googled the club name and found the address. "It's on South Broadway, near Evans. I remembered going there a long time ago, when the club had a different name. What was it?"

"Beats me," Cal said as he eyed the kitten warily. "I would never have gone there."

I laughed. "So true."

Cal came around the desk and peered over my shoulder. "What're you doing now?"

"Checking the website for the club."

The kitten leaped down and started playing with Cal's shoelaces.

"Hey," Cal said. "What're you doing?" He moved his foot back, which only made the kitten attack the shoelaces even more.

"Throw that mouse at him." I pointed at a toy mouse that I assumed Willie had got for him.

Cal grabbed the mouse and tossed it into the hallway. The kitten bounded after it.

"I'd be surprised if the website gives you any information about who owns it," Cal said.

"I would, too, but it's a place to start."

I poked around the website, with Cal looking on.

"See," he said. "I told you the website wouldn't list any owners."

I tried googling other search terms, like "Club 77 owner," but I still couldn't find any information.

"This could take you forever," Cal said as he grabbed his laptop.

"Hey, I'm trying."

He laughed as he started typing, and I kept my search going as he began his. In about five minutes, I hadn't come up with anything, but he turned his laptop to face me. "The club is owned by a group of investors."

I whistled. "That was fast," I said as I looked at a list of names. One was Rick Crabtree.

"That's him," I said.

Cal nodded. "His office is on Market Street, downtown."

"Great." I grabbed my phone and dialed the office number. A moment later, a woman gave me a cheery greeting, and I asked for Crabtree.

I heard a click, and then a deep voice said, "Rick Crabtree."

I told him my name, and then asked if he knew Gabe Culpepper.

"I do," he said.

"Are you aware that he was murdered two nights ago?"

"You're kidding." He seemed genuinely surprised. "What happened?"

I told him the barest details. "I'm a private investigator working on the case, and I'd like to ask you some questions about Gabe, and about a man who you both spoke to at Club 77."

"That could've been any number of people."

"I have his picture, and I'd like to show it to you."

"Okay, but I've got back-to-back meetings, and then I have to go to the club. Could you meet me there, say around two?"

"That'll work."

When I finished, I glanced at Cal. "Looks like I have some time to kill."

"Don't look at me. I've got to finish up a presentation for this afternoon."

I stood up. "Then I'll let you commandeer my office, and I'll get out of your way."

"Thanks," he said as he plopped into my just-vacated chair. The kitten had come back into the room, and he immediately jumped onto Cal's lap. Cal sat back, his arms in the air. "What do I do about him?"

"He's been playing for a while, so he'll probably go to sleep. Don't worry, he won't hurt you."

"Uh …" He shifted in his seat, but the kitten stayed put. Cal growled and started typing.

"See?" I said. "You're fine."

Before I made it to the door, Cal was already deep in thought as he typed away, oblivious to me and to the kitten, who had curled up and was already asleep.

CHAPTER EIGHTEEN

Since I didn't have to meet Rick Crabtree until two, I had some time to kill, and the first thing I decided to do was call the Silver Bullet Shooting Range. Phil answered.

"Reed, what are you up to? We haven't seen you in a while," he said, his voice booming.

"It's been a little crazy," I said.

"Working a case?" The guys there knew I was a private investigator.

"I am, and I've got a favor to ask. Has a woman named Sally Evans been in there before?"

"Hmm, let me think a second."

"She may have been in with a woman named Kristen Dalrymple."

"Oh, sure, I know Kristen. Nice young lady. And now I remember Sally. She came in with Kristen."

"Was Sally ever in by herself?"

"No, I don't think so, but let me check our records." He clicked his tongue while he checked. "No, she's only been in with Kristen. Why? Ah, never mind. You can't tell me, right?"

"Sorry."

"No worries."

"One other thing. Was Sally a good shot?"

"She did pretty well. The only reason I remember is they showed me their targets. You know, young gals, new with guns, kind of proud of themselves."

"Gotcha. Thanks, you've been a big help."

"You bet. I'll see you later."

I next called Spillman about my Glock. She said that ballistics tests had been completed, and that my Glock hadn't been used to murder Gabe Culpepper. Like I didn't know that. I thanked her and put my phone in my pocket. Then I hollered to Cal that I was leaving, but heard no reply. I smiled, knowing he was hard at work, and left. My first stop was at the police station to retrieve my gun, and then I went to Jones Transportation, where Sally worked. With everything that had gone on the previous day, I'd never managed to make it there.

Jones Transportation was located off Interstate 70 and Quebec Street, near where Denver's old airport used to be. I drove north on Quebec, where much of the area had been redeveloped, but ended up in an industrial area. I turned off Quebec and meandered east until I saw a small tan building with green trim. A sign on a post read "Jones Transportation." A wire fence surrounded a lot behind the building, and several trucks were parked near a large warehouse. I parked on a wide street and entered the tan building.

Inside was an unassuming office with two metal desks and a door that led to what I assumed were more offices and the warehouse. Other than that, there were only a couple of chairs against a gray-painted wall. A woman about Sally's age was sitting at one of the desks, typing at a computer. She was alone. She took earbuds out and set them near her cell phone, then straightened her dark hair.

"Hello," she said in a low voice.

I glanced at the other desk, then back to her. I introduced myself and said, "Sally Evans said I might stop by."

She made a show of giving me the once-over. "Oh, you're the detective."

"Right." I came over to her desk. "Did she tell you what's going on?"

She nodded, glanced over her shoulder to the door, then murmured. "But I haven't told anyone else."

"Sally said she asked for a leave of absence."

She primped her hair with her hands and gave me a little smile. "That's right. The boss likes her, so he was understanding."

I pointed toward the door. "Is the boss here?"

"Actually, he's not. But I can make an appointment if you'd like."

I shook my head. "That's okay."

She turned away from her computer, leaned her elbows on the desk, and rested her chin on linked hands. "Is Sally okay?"

She didn't seem in any hurry to get back to her work. I pulled over a chair and sat down across from her.

"She's all right," I said. "Do you mind if I ask you a few questions?"

"It's a little slow now, so sure. I'll do anything to help Sally."

"Let me be blunt," I said in a low voice. "Do you think Sally is capable of murder?"

"No way. She's too nice a person."

"Did you ever meet Gabe, her boyfriend?"

"Yeah. Now *he* was not a nice guy. Very arrogant, and he didn't treat her well."

"Oh?"

"He was using her."

"How so?"

She gnawed at her lip. "Call it a gut feeling. I mean, I think she was mainly with him because she thought he could help her produce some songs and videos, and she said that he encouraged her to write stuff down, like song lyrics and ideas. But then he took her notebooks and wouldn't give them back. That really made her mad." She thought for a moment. "I wondered if deep down he thought she had the talent, and he could use that to his advantage."

"How so?"

"Like … I don't know."

"The people I've talked to thought Gabe's music was good."

She shrugged. "It was all right, I guess, at least what I heard."

"And she was mad when he wouldn't give her notebooks back."

"Yeah." She held up a hand. "But it's not like she would kill him."

"How do you know?"

"Come on, that's extreme."

"They didn't get along well, and he was cheating on her."

"Yeah, but …" Her voice trailed off.

"But?" I prodded.

"It was just weird. It wasn't like he loved her or anything, and she knew that."

"Was he abusive toward her?"

She hesitated. "I think they fought. Honestly, I don't know why she stayed with him."

"That seems to be the general consensus." I jerked a thumb toward the other desk. "She's been working here for a month?"

"Yes. She's done some temp work now and again, and she does good work, so they decided to give her a try full-time."

"She's reliable?"

"Yes." She laughed. "I know, you've heard Sally's a flake, right?"

I nodded.

"Well, she is, sometimes, because I've seen her outside of work. But in here," she waved a hand around, "she does a great job."

"How long have you known her?"

She tapped a manicured finger on her cheek. "Let's see. I guess about three or four years. I met her at a club."

"Have you seen her perform?"

"A time or two, but I don't think she does that much anymore." She laughed. "She's not a bad singer, but comedy is where she excels. I think she should move to New York and get on with Saturday Night Live or something like that."

"Really?"

"Uh-huh. But she just doesn't seem to have the drive necessary, and she doesn't see herself as funny. Hmm, maybe her not being aware of herself is part of what makes her so funny." She sighed. "At least that's my take, but what do I know? I'm stuck at a dead-end office job."

"You really seem to like Sally."

"I do."

The phone rang. She answered it, took a message, and then looked at me. "I probably should get back to work."

I stood up. "Thanks for your time. I appreciate it."

"Anytime. Tell Sally 'hello from Angel' and to hang in there."

"I'll do that."

I put the chair back, waved at her, and left.

CHAPTER NINETEEN

I still had a lot of time to kill before I met Rick Crabtree, so I went by CJ's Auto Repair. Davon's Trans Am was parked in the lot near the shop. I took a spot down the street and watched for him. At noon, he emerged from the shop and I followed him to a Taco Bell on Colorado Boulevard. He sat inside, ate, and then drove to an apartment complex off Colorado and Colfax Avenue. I stayed down the street and watched as he drove slowly through the parking lot.

What's he doing? I wondered.

I didn't get an answer, as Davon left. By one o'clock, he was back at work. I parked in a different place, and was about to leave for my appointment with Rick Crabtree when Deuce called.

"Hey, Reed," he said in a low voice.

"What's up?"

"I took over for Ace a while ago, and I've been watching Sally's apartment."

"She's still there?"

"No, that's why I called. She left and I'm following her."

"Why're you whispering? She can't hear you."

"Oh, uh, okay."

"Where's she going?" The second it was out of my mouth, I knew

I should've rephrased it.

"How would I know that?" he said. "I didn't talk to her."

"Which way is she headed?"

"Oh. She's going north on York."

"Huh. That's not the direction where her mother lives."

"I've let some cars get between her car and my truck," he said. "I don't think she knows I'm behind her."

"Okay, stay with her and let me know what happens."

"Will do."

"I'm doing good, right?"

I smiled. "Yes, you are."

"Okay, I'll call you later," he said.

I put my phone away and left for my meeting with Rick Crabtree, but my mind was on Sally Evans. What was she up to? I'd told her the cops might have her under surveillance, and that she shouldn't go anywhere, except to visit her mother. Was she meeting her mother somewhere? If not, she apparently wasn't too impressed with my advice.

I shook my head. I'd find out later from Deuce where she went, and then I'd talk to her about it. I only hoped she wasn't doing something that would get her into more trouble.

» » » » »

Club 77 was located in a nondescript building tucked between a storage facility and an auto parts store on Evans, east of Colorado Boulevard, and if you didn't know it was a nightclub, you'd drive right by, thinking it was a small, rundown office building. The club was painted charcoal gray and had lots of colorful graffiti on the walls, with high windows covered in black paint.

Back when I'd gone there, during breaks when I was in college, I'd never paid much attention to the building itself. I liked the club because they'd had great, friendly deejays who spun new wave and alternative '80s music. Going there had been a rebellion of sorts for me against my well-to-do upbringing. I loved the punk crowds with their colorful outfits and crazy hair – who can forget the rattail or Mohawk – to the chagrin of my parents, who saw me shed my nice shirts and slacks for holey jeans, bright shirts, and a leather coat.

I parked in an empty lot on the side of the building and walked up to the front entrance, but the door was locked. I knocked, then tried to listen for noise inside, but the traffic sounds from the busy streets drowned out anything I might've heard. I finally gave up and walked around the side of the building. At the rear was another lot, and a few cars were parked there, including a black Mercedes. At the back of the building was an open door. I stepped into a kitchen where a man with beefy arms was loading a keg onto a dolly. He glanced up at me, but didn't stop working.

"We're closed."

"I'm looking for Rick Crabtree," I said. "I have a meeting with him."

He jerked a thumb at a door behind him. "He's in there."

I thanked him as I walked by. I pushed through the door and entered into the main part of the club, then glanced around. Square tables with stools lined the perimeter of a dance floor that seemed incredibly small. The walls were painted black, and dim overhead lights left the place in shadows. A stale odor lingered in the air. I'd never realized that without the pulsing music and darkness punctuated by a myriad of colored and strobe lights, the place was left with a dingy feel.

Voices drifted across the dance floor, and I looked toward a deejay booth at one end of the room. Inside the booth were two men. I crossed the floor and had a momentary flashback to being on the dance floor, my favorite '80s tunes playing loudly, the lights flashing to the beat, bodies gyrating rhythmically. That was a great time in my life. The men's conversation brought me back to reality.

"Yeah, do this set first." This from an older man in khakis and a short-sleeved polo shirt.

A young man in jeans and a T-shirt said, "Gotcha."

The older man glanced up and saw me. "Are you Reed?"

"I am," I said.

He gestured at the man in the T-shirt. "I'll catch up with you later." He came over and shook my hand firmly. "Rick Crabtree."

"Thanks for taking the time to meet with me," I said.

"No problem. Why don't you come into the office and we can talk there."

I followed him across the dance floor, through the kitchen, and down a short hall to a tiny room that was an office in name only. Shelves and boxes lined two walls, and a table and two folding chairs were against another. Posters of bands adorned the remaining wall. Rick pulled out the folding chairs and indicated that I should sit in one while he took the other. He crossed his leg, adjusted the collar of his shirt, and looked at me.

"I was surprised to hear about Gabe," Crabtree said. "He deejays for me sometimes. What happened?"

I told him, and explained that I was looking into the murder, but I didn't tell him who my client was.

"Wow," he said. "I can't believe that happened to Gabe."

"How well did you know him?" I asked.

"Mostly from his working here." He thought for a moment. "I guess he started deejaying here a couple of years ago."

"Was Gabe a good employee?"

He nodded. "I never had any trouble with him." His tone indicated something more.

"But what?" I asked.

He hesitated, then brushed a hand over thinning hair. "Gabe had a tendency to rub people the wrong way, but I didn't put up with any of that here."

"Do you know of any enemies he had?"

"Enemies?" He lips formed a grim line. "These young kids can get bent out of shape over nothing, so maybe Gabe crossed the wrong person, but who – I don't know."

"I know Gabe had some kind of altercation with this man." I pulled out my phone and showed him the picture I'd taken of Gabe and the man at the Rat Tavern. "Do you know him?"

Crabtree's eyebrows rose. "That's Chase Walker." He stared at me. "I can't imagine he's a suspect."

"Why not?"

"He's an investor in some clubs, and he represents some of the local talent. He's well-respected in the business community. I've known him for years. I even hooked him up with Gabe."

That got my attention. "How so?"

"Gabe had been talking to me for a while about finding someone to represent him."

"Represent in what way?"

"His music." Crabtree tapped the table for emphasis. "Gabe was creating some pretty good stuff lately, and he was hoping to find someone who'd take him on. Chase has connections with people in the recording industry, and I thought he might be able to help Gabe." His lips twitched into a reluctant smile. "To tell you the truth, I was getting tired of Gabe bugging me about how good he was and that he just needed the right break. And he was also talking about how he had something that was really big, and he kept saying how great it was. He kind of wore me down, and I called Chase and had him get in touch with Gabe. I didn't know if it would go anywhere, but at least it got Gabe to shut up."

"Was Gabe that good?"

He shrugged. "I liked his stuff, but I think it was this other thing that he was talking to Chase about."

"You have no idea what that meant?"

"I assume he meant some new songs, but all these guys," he waved a hand to encompass the club, "get competitive, and they worry that someone else is going to steal their sound. So Gabe was protecting whatever he thought he had."

Did Gabe and Chase meet here?"

"Yeah, about a month ago."

"Do you know if Chase was able to help out Gabe?"

He shook his head. "I don't talk to Chase much, and all Gabe said is that things were moving forward." He sat back and his chair creaked. "I just can't see Chase doing anything to harm Gabe, though. Chase is pretty laidback."

"I saw him with Gabe at a bar called the Rat Tavern. Their meeting didn't end well."

"Never heard of it." He frowned. "Gabe can push people's buttons, but I still don't see Chase committing murder. No way."

"Duly noted," I said. "Would you mind giving me Chase's

number?"

"He works at Walker Enterprises. It's downtown, and the number's on their website."

"I'll look it up." I thought for a second. "And there's no one else you can think of who might've had it in for Gabe?"

He rubbed his chin. "No, I'm sorry."

"No problem."

"Did you know Sally Evans?"

"Was she the woman that hung around with Gabe? She's a little bit older than he is?"

"That's her."

"Gabe mentioned her, but only in passing. I don't know much about her at all."

"Was she here the night Gabe and Chase met?"

"Yes, but she wasn't in on their conversation."

That confirmed what Sally had told me. "You seem pretty sure about that."

"Yeah, I remember because she hooked up with another guy."

"Who?"

"I don't know his name."

"What'd he look like?"

"Some scrawny kid who was too young for her."

I thought about that for a second. Sally had said that Gabe had been cheating on her, but had she been doing the same thing to him? Did it matter?

"Did Gabe know that Sally and this other man had hooked up?" I asked.

He shrugged. "I don't have a clue. By the time Gabe wrapped up his meeting with Chase, that other guy was gone. Sally and Gabe had a fight, and I told them to take it outside. She told him to go to hell and she took off. I assumed their fight was because of this other guy, but who knows? I could be wrong."

"I'm impressed with your memory."

He laughed. "Only because I'd come in that night to introduce Gabe to Chase. Otherwise, I wouldn't have been around." He glanced at his watch. "Hey, I've got to head out. I don't mean to cut you short, but …"

I handed him a business card. "If you think of anything else that might be helpful to me, I'd appreciate a call."

"You bet." He pocketed the card, stood up, and let out a long breath. "Sometimes I feel like all I do is run around."

I stood up and followed him out of the office. "I know the feeling."

He smiled. "I'll bet you do."

He led me through the kitchen and out the back, and as I walked around the side of building, I saw him go to the Mercedes. He hopped in and peeled out of the lot. When I reached the front, the Mercedes drove by on the street, and Crabtree was staring at me.

CHAPTER TWENTY

I sat in my car for a minute, pulled out my phone, and looked up Walker Enterprises. As Rick Crabtree had said, it was located downtown, and the office number was on the company website. I dialed it and asked to speak to Chase Walker.

"He's not in at the moment. May I take a message or put you through to his voice mail?" a pleasant female voice asked.

"Voice mail is fine," I said.

"One moment."

There was a pause, and then a clipped male voice said, "This is Chase Walker. I'm away from my desk. Leave a message and I'll get back to you as soon as I can." A beep followed. I left my name and number, and asked that Chase return my call about a very important matter involving Gabe Culpepper. Then I stuffed my phone back in my pocket and left Club 77.

I hadn't had a chance to get lunch, and I stopped at a Jimmy John's on Colorado Boulevard. While I ate, I texted Willie to let her know that I'd be working until later in the evening. Then I called Brenda Evans.

"Hello, Reed," she said. "How are things going?"

"I'm making some progress, but that doesn't mean I've been able to clear Sally yet."

"I know. And I know you're suspicious of her, but she didn't do this. I only hope you find out something soon, and we'll all know the truth. The stress is getting to me." She sounded tired. "But it's been good to reconnect with my daughter, although I wish the circumstances were different."

"I understand. Have you seen Sally much?"

"She was here yesterday for a while. It ... hasn't been easy in some ways, but we're catching up on lost time."

"What about today?"

"Not yet. She might come over for dinner."

"That sounds like a good plan," I said. "I'll touch base with you soon."

"Thank you."

I ended the call, and immediately called Deuce.

"Hey, Reed," he said cheerily. "What's up?"

"Where are you?"

"I was just going to call you. Sally went to an apartment building on Columbine. She's been inside for a while. I'm parked down the street."

"She used to live in the corner unit. Did she go there?"

"No, she went into the main door, but I didn't follow her, so I don't know which unit. You want me to find out?"

"No, don't blow your cover."

"My cover?"

I smiled. "You don't want her to see you."

"Oh, right. You want me to keep watching her?"

"If you have time."

"Sure. But this is getting kind of boring. Ace and I want to go play pool tonight."

"I know what you mean," I said. "I'm going to be watching someone myself."

"Ugh, no more for me after today. Is that all right?"

The Goofballs wanted to be involved in my investigations, right up until the time they got bored. Then, they were pretty much out. I didn't blame them, really. They were doing me a favor, and a lot of the time, investigations *were* boring.

"Watch her as long as you can, okay?" I said. "And I'll take you both to play some pool when I wrap up this case."

"Awesome. Hey, she's coming outside now," he whispered. "I'll follow her and let you know where she goes."

I shook my head. He would never figure out that people couldn't hear him when he was in his car.

"Great, thanks," I said, but he'd already ended the call.

I chuckled as I put my phone away. I finished my lunch and headed to CJ's Auto Repair. I verified that Davon's Trans Am was in the parking lot, then I parked in a different place than I had before and watched the shop. It was hot outside, summer not ready to yield to fall's cooler weather. I rolled down my window and waited. Time crept slowly by. At 4:45 Bogie spoke and I jumped.

"Hello?" I answered tentatively, not recognizing the number.

"This is Chase Walker."

"Thanks for returning my call."

"No problem. Rick Crabtree called me as well. I was shocked to learn Gabe had been murdered." He sounded genuinely concerned. "Rick said you might be calling me. Is there something I can help you with?"

"I'd like to talk to you about Gabe Culpepper, if you have some time, but not over the phone."

"Uh, sure, let me see. Could you come down to my office tomorrow, say around ten?"

"I'll be there."

I thanked him and no sooner had I put my phone back than Deuce called.

"Hey, Sally went back to her apartment."

"Thanks for letting me know," I said.

"You're sure you're okay if we don't watch her again tomorrow?"

"It's fine," I said. "I'll be visiting her at some point anyway, so no need for you to be there as well. Have fun playing pool."

"Thanks."

With that, he was gone.

I sat back and resumed watching the shop. Six o'clock finally arrived. Shortly after that, Davon emerged from the shop, retrieved his car, and drove away.

I followed him to the Rat Tavern, found a spot down the street, and again waited. Shortly after Davon went inside, the bald man that Davon had met the previous night showed up and strolled into the bar. I stretched, and waited, feeling the sentiments of the Goofballs. This was no fun. Finally, at dusk, Davon and his friend emerged from the bar.

They chatted for a minute on the sidewalk, then each went to his car and left. I was about to follow Davon when I saw a black SUV tear down the street, chasing the Trans Am. The bald man was driving. I let the SUV get ahead and tailed it. Farther up, I could see Davon's car. They drove to Davon's apartment, where Davon parked his Trans Am. He got out, donned a hoodie that he retrieved from his car, then hopped into the SUV. I was on their tail as they headed to Colorado Boulevard and went north.

It was dark when the SUV turned onto Colfax, and I suddenly had an idea where they were going. The SUV went a few blocks and turned onto a side street. I'd flicked my headlights off, pulled over at the corner, and peered down the street. The SUV had parked at the curb in front of the apartment complex where Davon had been this afternoon. Davon got out of the SUV, glanced around, then hurried into the parking lot.

I shut off the 4-Runner and grabbed my binoculars. Then I got out and quietly closed the door. I stayed in the shadows, crouched down, and hurried down the block. I stopped by a big truck and peeked over the hood. The SUV was farther up the street, its engine running. I focused the binoculars on the parking lot. It was illuminated by a few streetlights, but no one was about. Then I spotted Davon. He sauntered up to an older model Honda Accord, glanced around, then pulled something from his pocket. He went to the driver-side door, and although I couldn't *see* him, I *knew* what he was doing – breaking into the car. Seconds later, he had the door open and he vanished from view. Then the door closed and the Accord backed up.

I ducked down and ran back to the 4-Runner. By now, the Accord had pulled into the street, and the SUV followed it back to Colfax. I tailed them again, being extremely cautious. Davon drove to Interstate 70 and headed east to Quebec. The SUV stayed right with him.

We were now in a part of town that had a lot of warehouses and business complexes. I kept my distance as the two cars turned north, but when they turned onto Sandcreek Drive, where there were several warehouses nearby, I kept going. There was not enough traffic around the warehouses at that time of night, and I didn't want to be so conspicuous. I made a U-turn at the next light, then turned on Sandcreek.

I flicked off my headlights and drove down the street, then meandered up and down the next few blocks, but I didn't see the Accord. Disappointed, I headed back to Quebec.

I parked at a 7-Eleven to the north where I could watch Sandcreek Drive. I wasn't sure if I'd see Davon and his pal again, but I had a pretty good guess that a chop shop was located in one of the warehouses in the area, and that Davon was dropping off the stolen Accord there.

About the time I was ready to give up, an SUV appeared. As it passed under a streetlight, I could see the bald man, and Davon in the passenger seat. I assumed that they'd dropped off the Accord somewhere. I wondered how much Davon and his buddy got for the car they'd stolen.

I thought back to my conversation with Luis Hernandez, and how he'd overheard Davon arguing with Gabe about selling something, and threatening Gabe if he told anyone. Had Gabe been involved with Davon in stealing cars? It was a safe guess. But if Davon had killed Gabe, the question was why?

I shelved that thought as the SUV turned south. I tailed it, wondering if they were going to go after another car, but the SUV drove directly to Davon's apartment building without stopping. Davon got out and said something to the driver, and then the SUV headed away. I was about to follow it when Davon walked to his Trans Am, hopped in, and sped away. I decided to continue tailing him. He made his way to Hampden Avenue, went west, and turned into a shopping center just west of Broadway. He pulled into a space outside an IHOP, then moseyed inside. He had apparently been oblivious to me the entire night. But I was about to change that.

CHAPTER TWENTY-ONE

It was almost eleven, and the restaurant was nearly empty when I walked in. Davon was seated at a booth near the back, reading a menu. I went up to the booth and slid into the seat across from him. He jerked his head up in surprise, then recognition dawned on his face.

"What the hell are you doing here?" he snarled.

I gave him a big smile. "We need to talk."

"Get lost."

I settled back into the seat, indicating that I wasn't going anywhere. Then I pointed at him.

"You've been a bad boy."

Wariness flickered in his eyes. "Huh?"

"You lied to me."

"About what?"

"Your alibi, for one. I talked to your grandmother. But then, you know that."

He studied me carefully and shrugged. "So what?" He leaned forward. "You need to leave now."

Right then, a middle-aged waitress came up to the table. "You ready to order?"

"I'll have the double blueberry pancakes and a glass of milk," I said, then grinned at Davon. "What'll you have?"

Davon glared at me. The waitress sensed the tension in the air and her eyes darted between us. She stood with her pen poised over her order pad, not sure what to do.

"Hon?" she finally said to Davon.

"I'll have the burger with fries and a Coke." He handed her the menu, but still stared at me.

"Good choice," I said as the waitress ambled away.

"What do you want?" he hissed.

I jerked a thumb toward the kitchen. "Dinner – er, well, breakfast. Don't you like restaurants that serve breakfast at dinner?"

He wasn't sure what to make of me, so he stayed silent. I leaned toward him.

"You've been stealing cars," I said. He opened his mouth to protest, and I held up a hand. "Don't bother lying about that, too. I just saw you and your buddy with the SUV steal a Honda Accord."

His face went pale. I let him sit with that knowledge for a bit.

"You going to turn me in?" he asked.

"If I were going to do that, I wouldn't be having dinner with you." That was a lie. I was going to turn him in, but not until I talked to him first.

"What do you want?"

"What was going on between you and Gabe? The truth this time, or I *will* go to the police, and then you'll end up back in prison."

The waitress returned with my milk and his Coke. He took a long drink, then set the glass down.

"You know I've done time," he said.

I nodded. "I know a lot about you and your past. And I know there was something going on between you and Gabe."

"I didn't kill him."

"Remember, your alibi's not good. Was that because you were stealing cars the night Gabe was murdered?"

He hesitated, then nodded. "I couldn't tell you what I was really doing."

"No kidding." I took a sip of my milk and thought about him and Gabe, and what I knew. "Sally said she overheard you and Gabe talking, and he didn't want that action with you anymore. And a neighbor of Gabe's overheard you arguing with him. He said you were really mad at Gabe and you threatened him, and said Gabe better not tell anyone."

He grabbed a salt shaker and began fiddling with it. "So?"

"Let me take a guess, you and Gabe were stealing cars."

He stared at the salt shaker, and it took him a long time to answer. "Yeah."

"Why were you threatening Gabe?"

"He said he had another way of making money, that it was going to be big. He said he didn't need to steal cars anymore, that he couldn't risk getting into any kind of trouble. I told him he couldn't bail on me, and he laughed and said I should get a life." He snorted. "Can you believe that little punk was trying to tell me what I should do? I told him he didn't just get to walk away, and that we were in this together. He told me to leave him alone, and if I didn't, he'd call the cops on me. That's when I threatened him."

"Why were you messing around with him if you thought he was a punk?"

"Gabe was really good at stealing cars." A little smile crept across his face. "He was fast, and knew what he was doing."

Something else occurred to me. "You had the connections to the chop shops, so you'd let him steal the cars, and you knew where to sell them. You went together, but he actually stole the cars. But if he got caught, you'd drive off and leave him hanging."

He wouldn't make eye contact, and I knew I'd hit the nail on the head.

"That never happened," he said.

"Some friend," I muttered.

Now he glared at me. "Look, he got a split of some really good cash. And I was fair with him, even though I coulda taken more."

"Because you had the connections."

"Yeah."

"Where'd you steal the gun?" I asked, trying to catch him off-guard.

"What gun?"

"The Glock."

"I don't know what you're talking about."

If he knew that was the gun that had killed Gabe, he wasn't showing it. I thought for a moment.

"Had you heard any of Gabe's music?" I asked. "Was he that good?"

"I don't know. He was an okay deejay, got lots of girls. He'd try to play me some of his stuff, and it was all right, I guess."

Not an enthusiastic endorsement.

I stared at him. "You know something else."

His eyebrows furrowed. "I think this big thing he had going on was with a friend of his."

"Who?"

"Beats me. But sometimes he'd say *we* got some deal going, not *I* have some deal going. And one time he was talking about if he could work it to get all the money himself, he'd be rich."

"How would he do that?"

He shrugged and looked away.

I thought about something he had said in our first conversation. "You have the gambling problem, right? And you need cash fast."

He turned red.

"Gabe didn't owe you any money, did he?" I asked.

He shook his head.

"And now you've got a new guy to work with," I said, "but you're better at stealing cars than he is."

"He'll learn."

"Who is he?"

"I'm not telling you his name."

"But he's not as good as Gabe was."

He shrugged. "No."

The waitress brought our meals and set them down. When she left, I clapped my hands together.

"Boy, this looks good," I said with a grin. Davon glared at me. I dove into my pancakes and took a big bite. "Hmm, that's good." I pointed at him with my fork. "You should try yours."

"You're a real smartass," he said as he picked up his burger.

"I try."

The truth was, I was famished, and I ate quickly while we talked.

"How'd you meet Gabe?" I asked.

"Clubbing."

"And that led to a mutual interest in stealing cars."

He didn't say anything to that, but took a bite of his burger.

"When we first talked, you tried to steer me in the wrong direction," I said.

"I knew I had to say something to you. If I ran, you'd be suspicious."

"Turns out I was anyway. And you knew Gabe had been murdered."

"I told you, when you came to CJ's asking about Gabe, it was easy to figure out that something had happened to him."

"I see," I said, although I wasn't sure I believed him. "Who's Gregory Reichs?"

His jaw dropped. "How do you know about him?"

"I know more than you think."

"He's just a guy I know, and I'm hanging at his place for a while."

"Laying low? Don't want the cops to find you?"

He could tell I was still suspicious of him, but shrugged as if he didn't care, took another bite, and chewed slowly. "Now what?"

I shoveled the last of my pancakes in my mouth, then downed my milk. "I'm going to find out who killed Gabe," I said as I set down my glass. "If it was you, I *will* find that out."

He swallowed hard. "I was pissed off at him, but I didn't kill him. I don't want no murder rap."

"We'll see." I wiped my hands on my napkin and stood up. "Thanks for dinner."

I could feel his eyes boring into me as I walked out of the restaurant.

CHAPTER TWENTY-TWO

My mind was on Davon Edwards as I drove home. I felt as if he'd been telling the truth about his association with Gabe, but I wasn't sure I bought his alibi for the night Gabe Culpepper had been murdered. The problem was, I had no way of checking Davon's alibi, since it involved his stealing cars. I shook my head in frustration. I wasn't ready to eliminate him from my suspect list, since I had no way of proving that he hadn't killed Gabe. I was back to square one.

As I listened to some music, I wondered what big deal Gabe had going, and who knew about it. I'd add that to my list of questions to ask Sally, along with why she was at her old apartment building earlier today. I glanced at the dashboard clock. After eleven. Too late to call her now.

When I got home, the condo was dark. As I tiptoed down the hall, a tiny shadow leaped out of the darkness and almost tripped me. I reached down and picked up the kitten.

"Hey, little guy," I whispered.

He meowed and batted at my hand. I petted him as I went into the bedroom. Willie was asleep. I quietly undressed and crawled under the covers, trying not to disturb her, but the kitten crawled around her hair, and it didn't matter. Willie sighed and turned over.

"Hey," she said sleepily as she put an arm around me. She pulled the kitten close to her with her other hand.

"Hi." I leaned over and kissed her.

"How'd your day go?"

I filled her in, and when I finished, she said, "I've hardly seen you the last couple of days."

"I know, I'm sorry. Do you have to work tomorrow?"

She shook her head.

"How about a nice breakfast then? I'll cook," I said. "I have a meeting, but not until ten."

"That'd be great."

We lapsed into silence, and soon she was breathing deeply, the kitten snuggled by her head. I tried to stay awake and think about the case. I was missing something, I just couldn't figure out what. Minutes ticked by, and then I heard a dog barking outside. I waited, but it didn't stop.

I finally got up, went to the window, and peeked through the blinds. A dark-colored car was parked down the street, its headlights off, but I spotted some light from the interior. I watched it for a minute, then went out into the living room, followed by the kitten. I opened the front door and stepped onto the porch. The kitten darted out and I scooped him up.

"Hey, stay here," I whispered.

From the porch, I could see the car down the street. Suddenly, the car's engine revved and it sped past my building and was gone. I watched the street for a minute, but nothing happened. The dog quit barking and an eerie silence followed. Was someone watching the condo, or was I being paranoid? I shrugged as I went back inside and made sure the door was locked. Then I tiptoed back into the bedroom. Willie hadn't moved. I put the kitten on her pillow, slipped under the covers, and I too was soon asleep.

》》》》》

As promised, I fixed Willie a nice breakfast of Eggs Benedict, Canadian-style bacon, and toast. While we ate, we chatted about the case, and about her work. She told me about some of the drama at the hospital, and then she turned the conversation to the kitten.

"I have a good name for him," she said as she scooped him up and put him on her lap. "I think you'll like it." She smiled mischievously.

I eyed her. "Oh yeah?"

"Humphrey."

"Humphrey?"

"I know how much you'd like to give him a film noir kind of name, and you talk to Bogie all the time –"

"Not all the time," I murmured.

"So you wouldn't want to name the kitten 'Bogie' because that would be confusing, but he could be Humphrey."

I studied the kitten. "He kind of looks like a Humphrey."

"Then Humphrey it is." She kissed his head and set him down. Humphrey dashed over to a bowl of kitten food and started eating.

We got up and started clearing dishes.

"Do me a favor," I said casually, in order not to worry her. "Keep an eye out for anyone suspicious in the neighborhood, okay?"

"I always do," she said as she cleaned up her dishes.

That gave me pause. "Really?"

She stopped rinsing her plate and looked at me. "When you're on a case, I'm always extra careful."

"Does that bother you?"

She thought about that. "Well, let's just say it's not always fun, but I knew what I was getting into when I fell in love with you."

I came over and kissed her. "I love you."

"I love you, too." She kissed me again, hard, then patted me on the behind. "Go on, don't worry about me."

I grinned. "You know, I don't have to leave right now."

"You're terrible."

But she put down the plate, grabbed my hand, and led me into the bedroom.

» » » » »

On my way to my meeting with Chase Walker, I called Detective Spillman to tell her about Davon Edwards. Since she was a homicide detective, she said she'd pass along the information.

"What have you turned up?" she then asked.

"Nothing yet."

"Ferguson," she said slowly.

"I don't have anything concrete, but when I do, I'll let you know."

"You better," she said. "And don't get into any trouble."

"I never do."

"Yeah, right." With that, she hung up.

I laughed as I put my phone away.

» » » » »

At ten I was walking into the three-story Ghost Building on the corner of Eighteenth and Stout. I'd always been fascinated with the building, thinking it might have gotten that name because the place was haunted, but it was actually built in the late 1800's for a man named Allen H. Ghost. I'd read that the building had been on Fourteenth and

Glenarm, but in the 1970's the stone façade structure had been removed piece by piece and stored for ten years before it was reassembled at its present location in Denver's downtown historic district. I had yet to hear of the new building being plagued with ghosts.

I took the stairs to the second floor and marched down the hall to Walker Enterprises, then entered into a small lobby where a woman was sitting at a glass-top desk. She looked up from her computer with a smile.

"How may I help you?"

I introduced myself. "I have a ten o'clock meeting with Chase Walker," I said.

"If you'll have a seat, I'll let him know you're here."

I sat down on a white couch that was all hard cushions and uncomfortable angles. I glanced around, noting the modern décor and sterile feel of the room, but I didn't have time to dwell on it because a man in black slacks and a purple shirt came down a short hall. I recognized him as the man I'd seen at the Rat Tavern.

"Chase Walker," he said as he came up to me.

I shook his hand, and he led me down the hall to his office. Its décor was similar to the foyer, and a large window had a view of the Federal Courthouse. I took a seat in a white chair facing Walker's metal-and-glass desk. Chase sat down at a black leather chair behind the desk and looked at me.

"I was sorry to hear about Gabe," he said as he sat back and put his palms together.

"Rick Crabtree told you about him?"

"Yes. You said you had some questions for me? Are you with the police?"

I shook my head. "I'm private."

"I see."

I glanced around at several awards and knick-knacks displayed on glass shelves on one wall. A few framed photos showed Walker posing with some local sports figures, including Von Miller. "I understand Gabe was looking for representation," I began.

"That's right. Rick put him in touch with me."

"What exactly were you going to help Gabe with?"

"I was looking to manage him and line up some business opportunities."

"What kinds of opportunities?"

He tapped his fingertips together as he talked. "I was working with some local companies and even a few national companies to see if they wanted to use Gabe to promote their products."

"Advertising? I thought Gabe was a musician, mostly techno, and that he was looking for an agent. What kind of advertising would work with that?"

He shook his head. "I wasn't going to help him with his music." I must've looked puzzled because he said, "Are you familiar with social media influencers?"

"I've heard the term," I said, "but do you mean people who help businesses with their social media presence, or people like Logan Paul and King Bach?"

"Those two," he said with a smile. "Some of these guys get so many fans, companies are willing to pay big bucks to have social media personalities pimp their products. Logan Paul was recently paid something like three hundred thousand to create a thirty-second video for Dunkin Donuts. Guys like him speak to the millennial generation."

I held up a hand. "Wait, Gabe was a social media personality?" That was news to me.

He hesitated. "Not exactly. Gabe came to me because he said he knew who one of these personalities is, and he wanted me to work with them."

"Them?"

"Gabe and his partner."

"Who was his partner?"

"I don't know."

"What personality are we talking about?"

"Gabe said he knew who Masta Dig is." He scooted forward in his chair and tapped the table. "See, Masta Dig wears a mask and no one –"

"Knows who he is," I interrupted. "But Gabe did?"

"That's what he said."

"Did you believe him?"

He shrugged. "Not at first, but he proved it to me."

"How?"

"He told me about a new Masta Dig video before it was released. When I saw the video, it was exactly how Gabe described it. And he had Masta Dig skype with me."

"But Masta Dig wore his mask."

He nodded. "I didn't know who he was."

"And they were looking for representation."

"Right. They were smart enough to know they had a good thing going, that they had a huge following that was growing every day. There were big bucks to be made if we could strike while the iron was hot."

"While they were popular."

"Exactly. If you wait too long, someone else might be the big thing."

"Did you get to the point of officially representing Gabe and his partner?"

He shook his head. "No. I told him I couldn't have any secrets, that I needed to know what was going on, and who his partner was. Gabe said he would talk it over with his partner and get back to me. In the meantime, I started working on some things on my end, setting up exploratory meetings with some companies. I had a company that was willing to pay them two hundred thousand for a thirty-second ad."

I whistled. "Not too shabby."

"Right."

"You were sure Gabe would get his partner to agree to meet with you, without the mask."

He nodded. "We're talking a lot of money for a kid who didn't appear to have much."

"I saw you meet Gabe at the Rat Tavern the night he was murdered."

He let out a little laugh. "Yes, not the best place to conduct meetings, but that's where he wanted it, so …" He shrugged. "Who was I to argue? Anyway, he was supposed to bring in his partner, but he didn't."

"Why didn't the partner come in?"

He frowned. "They said Masta Dig had to stay secret, that no one knowing who he really was is part of what makes it special. Gabe was almost joking about it, telling me that it wasn't a big deal, and that he'd handle everything. He was being a bit too cavalier for my taste."

"And you got angry."

He arched an eyebrow. "Oh, you saw that."

I nodded. "You weren't too happy with him."

"No, I wasn't. I'd been working for a while on this, seeing what interest there was in Masta Dig, but I told him there's no way I was working with them, unless I knew who I was dealing with, and neither were potential advertisers. Gabe said that wasn't going to happen, and he started telling me how I should run things. He really didn't understand business, and I felt like he was playing games with me, even though I'd taken him very seriously."

"And that made you mad."

"You bet it did."

"Gabe was the one calling the shots."

"Gabe was *trying* to call the shots. That's the way it seemed to me. As far as I know, he created the social media accounts and the website."

I remembered something else. "You gave him something at the bar."

"A USB drive with some videos that they'd created but hadn't posted yet."

He said it so matter-of-factly, I didn't think he was lying. "What did you do after you left the Rat Tavern?"

"I met some friends for dinner at Elway's and then stayed for drinks at the bar," he said. "I go there a lot, and the staff knows me."

Elway's is a pricey steakhouse that's owned by former hall-of-fame quarterback, John Elway, one of Denver's best-known personalities.

"Any problem if I go there and verify that?" I asked.

"No problem." He grabbed a business card from the desk, leaned forward, and handed it to me. "Ask for Sam Ainsley, and tell him to call me if that helps."

"Thanks," I said as I took the card and pocketed it.

He seemed sure about his alibi and not at all offended that I was asking for one. That either made him really slick, or he was innocent.

I thought for a second. "There was interest in having Masta Dig promote products?"

He nodded. "Oh yeah. A lot of companies understand that these personalities can reach the younger generation in a whole new way."

I changed topics. "Do you know anything about Gabe's girlfriend Sally?"

He pressed his lips together, puzzled. "That name doesn't ring a bell."

I described Sally. "She was at the club the night you met Gabe there."

"He had a number of women talking to him that night, but this particular woman …" He shook his head. "I don't recall seeing her."

"How often did you meet Gabe?"

"A handful of times. I saw him that time at Club 77, and he came down here once. Oh, and one other time at the Rat Tavern."

"When did you first meet with him?"

He sighed. "Oh, about a month ago."

Rick Crabtree had told me the same thing.

"And you have no idea who Masta Dig is?" I asked again.

He shook his head. "I think he was at the club the night I first met Gabe."

"Oh yeah?"

"Yes. I told Gabe that I should get to know his partner, and his partner should get to know me. Gabe laughed and said something about his partner was around and not a stranger. I had the feeling the partner was at the club." He shrugged. "It doesn't matter now, Masta Dig is gone, now that Gabe is."

"Along with the money to be made," I said, and watched his reaction.

"Yeah, but that's not the main thing, is it? A man lost his life."

"True."

Chase Walker seemed sincere about Gabe. And he'd been very forthcoming. He could've been doing that to throw me off, but my gut said that wasn't the case. I couldn't see any motive that he'd have for murdering Gabe. If Chase's alibi checked out, I'd likely cross him off my suspect list.

I stood up. "I appreciate your taking the time to talk to me."

"No problem."

He got up and walked me back to the main office. "If you have any other questions, don't hesitate to call."

"Thank you."

He smiled as he held the door open for me.

CHAPTER TWENTY-THREE

I mulled over my conversation with Chase Walker as I strolled to my car. Gabe Culpepper knew Masta Dig. But did that have anything to do with Gabe's death? That seemed crazy to me. Another thought kept coming to me. What did Sally know about all this, if anything? Had she helped Gabe in creating Masta Dig videos? Then, when things went bad between them, had she murdered him? That seemed crazy as well, but then, stranger things have happened. And who was Masta Dig? That man might be able to shed some light on Gabe's murder. But how to find him?

I didn't lose any time in calling Sally, so I could ask her those questions. Unfortunately, she didn't answer her phone. I left a message, asking her to return my call as soon as she got it. I swore at her as I crammed my phone in my pocket, then drove a few blocks to the Ritz-Carlton Hotel on Eighteenth and Curtis. Right next door was Elway's Restaurant.

I parked and paid the meter, then crossed Curtis. It wasn't quite eleven, and Elway's street entrance was still locked, so I went into the hotel lobby and around to the restaurant. I stepped into a shadowy foyer and looked around. The restaurant was decorated in dark tones, with dark wood-paneled walls and ceiling, and tables with brown leather chairs.

Soft music played from hidden speakers. A host in dark slacks and a white shirt saw me and approached.

"We're not open just yet," he said with a reserved smile.

"Yes, I know," I said. "I'm looking for Sam Ainsley. He's the –"

"Yes, he's in the back. If you'll wait here, I'll get him."

I nodded. The host turned and walked through the restaurant while I looked around. I had been to the Elway's in Cherry Creek, and even though this location was closer to the condo, I hadn't been here. I was just thinking I should bring Willie to this Elway's when a man in a dark suit walked up.

"May I help you?" he asked, his voice buttery smooth.

"I hope so," I said. "I was just visiting with Chase Walker, and he said you would be able to verify that he was here on Sunday night."

He gave me a funny look. "Well, I … sir, I can't disclose who our patrons are."

"I understand, but he said to give him a call and he'd okay it." I held out Walker's business card.

He hesitated, then took the card, staring at me the whole time. "Your name?"

"Reed Ferguson."

His lips formed a disapproving line as he moved around a small podium and picked up a phone. He glanced at the number on the card, dialed, and asked to speak with Chase Walker. Then he turned his head and murmured into the phone. I heard snippets of the conversation, mostly him describing me. He finally nodded and hung up.

"Mr. Walker said to answer any questions you have." He was being polite, but bemusement was etched on his face.

"Good," I said. "Chase said you could verify that he was here on

Sunday night," I repeated.

"That's correct."

"How do you know?"

"Mr. Walker comes in here most Sunday nights. Sometimes he's with friends, sometimes he dines alone. He's a very good customer."

"When did he arrive that night?"

"About nine o'clock. He had a late dinner with friends and then stayed at the bar until after eleven. Would you like to know what he had to eat?"

I ignored his not-so-subtle sarcasm. "Would anyone else remember Chase being here?"

"Of course. The bartender and Mr. Walker's waitress would remember, but they're not here now." He raised his eyebrows. "Would you like me to call them?"

"That's okay," I said.

I thought Ainsley was telling the truth, and I doubted that Chase Walker would've been able to get all these people to lie and say that he'd been here the night Gabe Culpepper had been murdered. As far as I was concerned, Chase's alibi was solid. There was no way he could've murdered Gabe at the same time he had been at Elway's. I thanked the host for his time and left.

I dashed across Curtis Street and got in the 4-Runner, but before I left, I tried Sally again. No answer. I growled, then pulled into traffic.

"Where are you, Sally?" I muttered as I turned the corner.

Since Sally lived close by, I headed there. I found a parking place on the corner of Humboldt, and as I walked down the steps to Kristen Dalrymple's apartment, rock music came from an open window. I knocked on the door and waited. When no one answered, I banged harder on the door, and it suddenly opened. Kristen looked up at me in surprise.

"Oh, hey. What's up?" She looked a little frazzled, her hair askew. The music was even louder now.

I glanced past her. "Is Sally around?"

She shook her head, then held up a hand. She darted into the living room and turned off the music. "I don't know where she is," she said as she came back to the door.

"When did she leave?"

"Well, I haven't seen her since yesterday."

I couldn't contain my surprise. "She didn't come home last night?"

"No, well, uh, I don't know. I saw her before I left for work last night. You know, here." She pointed behind her. "But I spent the night at my boyfriend's. When I got home this morning, Sally was gone. I figured she left before I got home."

"Did she leave a note saying where she went?"

"No. Sometimes we tell each other, but I don't keep track of her." She rolled her eyes. "I'm not her mother."

"Right, I get it," I said.

She shifted from foot to foot, and glanced over her shoulder. "Hey, listen, I gotta go, okay?"

I tried to look behind her. Was Sally there and she didn't want me to know? "Sure. If you see Sally, tell her to call me as soon as possible."

"Okay."

Kristen shut the door and as I walked slowly up the steps, I called Sally again and listened for a ring through the apartment window. I didn't hear anything, nor did Sally answer. Then the music started up again, as loud as before. I hurried to my car and called Brenda.

"Hello?" she answered, her voice tired.

"It's Reed Ferguson," I said. "Is Sally there?"

"She was, but she left."

"Where's she going?"

"I think she's headed home. Is everything okay?"

"She's not answering her phone."

She sighed. "That sounds like Sally. That girl…" She left the rest unsaid.

"If you talk to her, tell her to call me. It's important."

"I will. Have you found out something?"

I hesitated. "I'm not sure yet."

"Sally didn't do this. Trust me, a mother knows."

"Uh-huh. I'll call you when I know more."

She thanked me and was gone. I sat back, cranked some tunes, and waited. A few minutes later, Kristen came out and strode down the street away from me. She got into a green car, pulled into the street, and turned the corner.

I waited for an hour, and as I did, I thought about Gabe and Masta Dig. *Who was that masked man?* I thought, conjuring up the old Lone Ranger movies. I went over all I knew about Masta Dig, which wasn't much. The Goofballs thought he was funny. And so did millions of others.

My mind went to Gabe's neighbor Luis Hernandez, and I mulled over my encounter with him. I remembered how much he seemed to like Gabe, and how much he knew about social media personalities. Did Luis know more than he'd told me? I stared out the window at dark clouds that were building in the west and thought about him. It'd be worth talking to him again. It would be better than wasting time waiting for

Sally to show up. I tried her again, but she still didn't answer. I swore and left. I'd try her later.

I drove to Race Street and parked. The wind picked up, whipping at my clothes as I rushed inside the vestibule. I pressed Luis's call button below his mailbox, but he didn't answer, so I hurried back to my car and watched the building. I was getting tired of all the waiting, but this time I didn't have long because Luis soon ran up the sidewalk. I got out of the car and raced up to the building. When I entered the lobby, the glass security door was closing. I grabbed the handle, flung the door open, and hustled inside. I heard Luis in the stairwell. I took the steps two-at-a-time and then saw him above me.

"Hey," I called out. "I need to talk to you."

Luis turned around and stared at me. Then he whirled around and dashed up the stairs.

CHAPTER TWENTY-FOUR

I swore as I bolted after him. When I reached the third floor, he was at his door, digging in his pocket. He looked up at me, then unlocked his door.

"I'm busy," he said as he hurriedly unlocked the door.

"What the hell!" I sprinted down the hall and reached his door just as he got it open.

He tried to slam it shut, but I put my shoulder into it, stopping him.

"Hey!" He tried to push the door shut, but I was bigger than he was, and he finally gave up.

"We need to talk," I said as I held the door open.

"I don't got nothin' to say to you."

"Tell me what you know about Masta Dig."

"No."

"Are you Masta Dig?" I asked.

He burst out laughing. "Hell no. You think I'd be working at a Burger King if I was? I'd be cashing in the dough."

"You know who he is."

He hesitated. "No."

I took a step forward. "Tell me what you know or I'll call the cops."

"And tell them what?"

"That you know something about Gabe Culpepper's murder. I have a friend who's a detective, and she'll make life miserable for you."

I was bluffing, but it worked.

"No, don't call anyone," he said.

He glanced up and down the hall, his eyes settling on the crime scene tape that was still stretched across Gabe's door. Then he stepped back to let me in. He sat on the couch, but I stayed standing near the door. I crossed my arms and stared at him. He drew in a breath and let it out slowly.

"Masta Dig might know something about Gabe's murder," I said, "so you need to tell me what you know."

"I don't know who Masta Dig is, but I've been around when they filmed some of their videos. I never saw Masta Dig without his mask."

"It is a man?"

He shrugged. "I guess. Who else would it be?"

"A woman with a deep voice?"

"Nah. It was a dude. Sometimes he had a little device that would distort his voice as he talked, but it was a man."

I thought for a second. "Why'd they let you come along when they shot these videos?"

"Gabe started showing me the videos and I thought they were hilarious, and we'd get to talking about Masta Dig. One time, Gabe was a little high, and he started bragging about how he knew Masta Dig." Luis swore. "I told him I didn't believe him, and that made him mad, but I just laughed it off. Then I saw him another time and he said he was going to meet Masta Dig and they were going to do some videos. He asked me to come along, and I did." A smile spread across his face. "It was awesome, man. They had some stuff written down, like a little script, and Masta Dig would do his thing, and Gabe filmed it. But man, I should've filmed the outtakes. Those were funny, too. Gabe would get mad at Masta Dig if he wasn't doing stuff right, and they'd argue. Gabe would be like 'Hey, eh, do it like this,' or 'You gotta go here, eh.' It was like he was Canadian, you know?"

"Uh-huh."

"It was so cool." His voice grew wistful. "I just wanted to be a part of it because they're gonna hit it big." Then he sat up straighter. "Actually, I was in a video or two."

"Oh yeah?"

He nodded. "Sometimes I'd be like the straight guy, and Masta Dig would ask me questions or things like that."

"And you hoped some day they'd pay you?"

"Well, yeah, only it never happened. But it was still cool to be in the videos."

"Maybe you wanted to be more involved, so you got Gabe out of the way."

He held up his hands and gestured at me to stop. "No! I don't know who Masta Dig is. They even laughed at me because they thought it was funny that Masta Dig's identity was secret."

I stared at him for a moment, and something in his eyes led me to believe him.

"Where'd they film the videos?" I asked. "Masta Dig wore a mask, so wouldn't that attract a lot of attention?"

"If they're in public, it does, but they film in private as well."

"Where?"

"They go to the mountains, or I've seen videos in some kind of warehouse, but the only place I've ever been is this old farmhouse east of town. I don't know how they knew about it, but we could film in the house, or the barn. And there was a big hill with a huge rock formation and we'd go there. Look, let me show you."

He got up quickly, and I braced myself, wondering if he was going to suddenly bolt past me. But instead, he grabbed his laptop off the desk, booted it up, and brought it over to me.

"Look," he said as he navigated to Masta Dig's YouTube channel. He found a video and clicked on it.

The video showed a long porch and just as it panned to the left, Masta Dig burst through a door.

"Hey, hey!" he said, and then launched into a brief rap. When he finished, Luis appeared from the right. They talked for a moment about a party they were going to, and Masta Dig poked some fun at Luis's expense, and that was it. It was short, and for whatever reason it seemed vaguely familiar. But it was not funny, in my opinion. However, the video had over two million views.

"Hilarious, right?" Luis said. "And that's me."

I pointed at the screen. "How do I find this place?"

"You go out I-76, and it's near Roggen. It's not hard to find."

Roggen is a small town about an hour northeast of Denver. I cocked an eyebrow at him and he gave me detailed directions.

"How often did they go out there?" I asked.

"I dunno. Lots of times, I guess." He put the laptop back on the desk.

"Is there anything else you can tell me about Masta Dig?"

He hesitated.

I eyed him hard. "What?"

"Man, I don't want to get involved."

"Too bad, you are." I was not in a sympathetic mood.

He gestured toward the door. "Since Gabe died, a couple of times when I've come home, some guy in a hoodie has been hanging around the hallway. I think he might be trying to get into Gabe's apartment."

Gabe had met someone at the McDonald's who wore a hoodie, too. And I'd seen Davon in a hoodie just last night. Coincidence that a man in a hoodie had been hanging around Gabe's apartment? I doubted it. But was it Davon?

"What'd he look like?" I asked.

"Not very tall, and I think he had dark hair, but it was hard to tell with the hoodie."

I went to the door, and as I put my hand on the knob, I tried to look stern. "If you're lying to me …"

"I'm not!" He stood with his feet apart, trying to look tough, but it wasn't working.

I gave him a curt nod and went out the door.

CHAPTER TWENTY-FIVE

I stopped by Sally's apartment again, but she still wasn't home, or she wasn't coming to the door. I called her cell, but she didn't pick up. She'd said she didn't always keep her phone with her, but this was ridiculous. I frowned. Was she doing her disappearing act again? Or, if she was guilty, maybe she'd taken off. Something else occurred to me. If she knew more about Masta Dig than she'd told me, did she know about the farmhouse in Roggen? Could she have holed up there? It'd be worth checking.

I stopped at Taco Bell for a late lunch, wolfed down a burrito, then picked up Interstate 76 and headed toward Roggen. Traffic was building, but it thinned some as I got farther from the metro area. Farmland was on either side of me, much of it still green. As I neared Roggen, lightning flashed across the sky and a moment later, a horrendous clap of thunder rocked the 4-Runner. Several big drops of rain hit the windshield but then stopped.

The directions that Luis had given me to the farmhouse weren't complicated. I turned off at Roggen – a tiny town without much of anything in it – and took Highway 73 south past Boulder Valley Poultry, a huge chicken farm. Beyond that was a large farm, and after another mile, I took a dirt road west. I drove until the road curved north. Nothing was out here except farmland. Then I saw a house in the distance. It sat at the end of the road, with fields all around. I stopped the 4-Runner, pulled the binoculars from behind the seat, and scrutinized the property.

The farmhouse was two stories, with a porch that ran the length of the house. The paint was peeling, the windows were broken, and some of the screens were torn and fluttering in the wind. Near the house was a small, weathered barn. I watched for a minute, but didn't see any cars or people about. I put the binoculars away and drove slowly up to the house. The storm clouds were so dark and heavy, it seemed like night.

I took my Glock and holster from under the seat and strapped it on, then got out and walked up sagging steps onto the porch. I tried to picture the video that Luis had showed me, and I moved to the spot where the cameraman had stood.

It definitely could've been filmed here, I thought.

The front door was shut, but not locked. I let myself in and called out. No answer. A musty odor assaulted my nose, and I coughed as I looked around. To the left was a living room, empty except for a rickety chair in the corner. A fireplace still held ashes of old burned logs. A few candy wrappers were strewn about the floor. Wind whistled through a broken window that looked out onto the porch. I pulled out my phone and tried to google Masta Dig, but I couldn't get a signal.

I took a few pictures, then put my phone away and moved into an empty dining area. On the wall someone had scratched the letters M and D. I took a picture of that as well, then stepped into a kitchen. I checked, but found nothing in the cabinets. I went to the sink and tried the faucet. No water. If Sally was holed up here, she hadn't left any food. I looked in another room on the main level before going upstairs.

Three upstairs rooms were also empty. I checked closets and found some old newspapers and footprints in dust that covered the floors. In a back room, I went to the window and peered out. About a hundred yards from the house was a hill and at the top was a large rock formation surrounded by dead shrubs. Everything was as Luis Hernandez had described it, but so far I wasn't finding anything that would help me figure out Masta Dig's identity. I traipsed back downstairs and found a door to the basement. I opened it and peered into the darkness.

"Sally?"

No answer.

I found a light switch and flicked it on, but nothing happened. Not that I expected it to. I went back to the 4-Runner and got a powerful flashlight from the glovebox, then went back into the house. I turned on the flashlight and tiptoed down the steps into the basement.

It was unfinished, with an old water heater and furnace in the corner. I shined the light around and saw nothing but cobwebs and dirt, but I walked around the room anyway, not sure what I was hoping to find. If Sally was staying here, I didn't see any evidence of it. I had stirred up dust, and I suddenly sneezed violently. I cleared my throat and when I finished, I thought I heard something. I listened, then went to a small window high up on the wall and looked out. All I could see was dark sky. A rumble of thunder shook the glass in the window. But was there something else? I flicked off the flashlight and tiptoed to the stairs. I listened as I peered up toward the kitchen.

Nothing.

I finally shrugged, trudged upstairs, and let myself out a back door. I trotted to the barn and checked it out. It was empty, but a white sheet had been hung on one wall. I peeked behind it, but it wasn't hiding anything. I went outside and jogged through the gloom across a barren field toward the rock outcropping. Lightning flashed, followed quickly by thunder, and it made me jump.

So unlike Bogie, I thought.

When I reached the rock outcropping, I looked around and saw where the earth had been trampled. Someone frequented this area.

The rock on the side nearest the farmhouse was a sheer, sloping face that would be hard to scale, but a beaten path went around the outcropping and I followed it. Thin tire tracks from what I guessed was a bicycle were evident. At the back side of the formation was a spot where I could scramble up the rock. I shoved the end of the flashlight as best I could into my pocket and climbed to the top of the rock and scanned the terrain. Corn fields were to the north, and alfalfa to the south. A spectacular view of the mountains was to the west. I admired it for a moment, then turned to look at the abandoned house. I wondered who owned it.

Light rain began to fall, and I started to climb down off the rock. The rain grew harder, and my footing slipped more than once. I was going to have to hurry before the fields were a muddy mess.

I reached the ground and was walking back toward the front of the outcropping when a crack rang out. I had an instant of wondering where the lightning had been, and then shards of rock hit my face. Just as another crack split the air, I had an instant realization that someone was shooting at me. I fell to the ground and listened. All I could hear was the wind. I reached down and pulled my Glock from my holster and waited. When nothing happened, I raised my head. I couldn't see anything. The rain grew harder and the wind picked up.

I finally got into a crouch and dashed in between shrubs and into the rows of tall corn, where I had better cover. A third shot rang out and I dove for the ground again. It was muddy and wet. I peeked through the corn stalks and thought I saw movement. I stared in that direction, thinking it might've been a man in a hoodie, but it could've been my imagination. I waited a second, got into a squat and pushed through the stalks, my gun aimed in front of me. I thought I heard the corn rustling up ahead, but with the rain and wind, I couldn't be sure. I made my way through the corn, and as I neared the farmhouse, I reached the edge of the cornfield. I bent down and looked out.

Off in the distance, red taillights winked in the gloom. I emerged from the corn and ran to the front of the house where the 4-Runner was parked. I hopped in and started it, then pressed on the gas. My wheels skidded back and forth in the mud, and then I rocketed forward. I circled around and drove fast, but I didn't see the taillights. I finally reached Highway 73, but I never saw another car. I hit the steering wheel in frustration, then took a moment to wipe my face off. I was soaked to the skin, muddy, and cranky. And I realized I'd lost my flashlight, but I wasn't going back to try to find it. I turned north and headed back to Denver, but my mind was on what had just happened at the farmhouse.

Someone hadn't liked my poking around the house. But who?

CHAPTER TWENTY-SIX

"What *happened* to you?" Willie asked when I walked through the door.

She had sample paint cards and she was holding them next to curtains she'd recently bought. Humphrey had been sleeping on the couch, and he got up, stretched, and then stared at me warily.

"I got caught in a field in the rain," I said as I stood by the door and shivered. I was a mess, with mud all over my front side and in my hair. Even walking through the rain from my car to the condo hadn't helped with the mud.

She cocked an eyebrow at me, and I started to tell her about my afternoon, but she held up a hand to stop me.

"Why don't you get out of those clothes and hop in the shower?" she interrupted as she came over.

"That's not a bad idea."

While I stripped off my clothes by the door, I told her everything that had happened since I'd left, except for getting shot at. No need to worry her. She took my clothes and threw them in the laundry room.

"I'm going to fix some lasagna for dinner," she said when I finished. "Maybe that and a shower will help warm you up."

"Sounds good."

She kissed me, then wiped her mouth. "I love you, babe, but you're a mess."

I laughed as I padded in my underwear to the master bath and took a shower. While hot water rushed over me, I thought about being shot at in the field. I was almost certain I'd seen someone in a hoodie. Had Davon Edwards gone to the farmhouse and used me for target practice? Was he Masta Dig?

My thoughts turned to Sally. She'd never mentioned Masta Dig, but was that because she'd never heard of him, or was she hiding something? I needed to talk to her, and I'd called her again on my way home from Roggen, but she hadn't picked up. I had no idea where she was, but I needed to find her after I cleaned up. I was starting to worry that she wasn't just being a flake by having her phone turned off, but that something bad had happened to her.

I finished showering, toweled off, and put on clean clothes, then went into the kitchen for a beer. I took a long gulp and watched Willie for a bit, but my mind was elsewhere. I finally asked, "Can I help with anything?"

Willie must've seen the distracted look on my face, and she shook her head. "You have some work to do, right?"

I nodded. "I need to look up some stuff on the computer, and then I need to find Sally Evans. She seems to be avoiding me."

She kept stirring the spaghetti sauce. "I've got this handled. Do what you need to do and I'll call you when dinner's ready."

I leaned over and kissed her. "Thanks."

She was humming as I went into my office. Humphrey jumped into my lap as I put my beer on the desk and logged onto the internet. I googled "Masta Dig" and found his YouTube and Vine channels. I absentmindedly petted Humphrey while I watched a few Masta Dig videos, but didn't see anything noteworthy, except the masks changed. Sometimes the eyebrows were heavy, sometimes the mouth was upturned, other times it looked like a frown. Other than that, it was a masked man with a voice that could've been anybody's. There wasn't anything particularly unique about his outfits, either. He was usually dressed in jeans and T-shirts, sometimes a hoodie, and the most distinctive thing about him was what appeared to be a tattoo on his left biceps, but I couldn't tell what it was. I did recognize the farmhouse and the rock formation in some of the videos. And in others, Masta Dig was standing in front of a white background, which appeared to be the sheet that I'd seen hung up in the barn.

After watching a few more videos – and still not seeing the humor in them – I went to Gabe Culpepper's Facebook page and poked around. He'd posted a lot of pictures of himself deejaying at clubs around the city, along with his music videos. I watched a few and read some of his posts, hoping to find some clue to Masta Dig's identity, but I didn't have any luck.

I glanced at Bogie's picture on the posters.

"How about some inspiration?" I said to him.

He looked cool, but he didn't say anything to me. Too bad. I picked up Humphrey and looked him in the eye.

"Do *you* have any inspiration for me?" I asked.

He meowed and his whiskers twitched.

"I don't know what that means," I said as I put him back in my lap.

I watched some more Masta Dig videos while I drank my beer, and Willie popped in a while later.

"Dinner's about –" She stopped when she heard some of Masta

Dig's shtick. "What in the world is that?"

I pointed at the monitor. "That," I said dramatically, "is Masta Dig."

She moved around so she could look over my shoulder. The video finished and I glanced at her. Her brow was wrinkled.

"What do you think?" I asked.

"Play another."

I did, and she looked even more bemused.

"I don't get it," she said. "This is funny?"

"To a lot of people. This dude has over five million followers on YouTube."

"Huh."

"The Goofballs like him."

"Oooh," she said, then watched another one. "I could see how Ace and Deuce would think that's funny."

"But you don't see it."

"Do you?"

I shook my head as another video began playing.

"Give me some of your '80s songs any day."

"This guy might make millions." I explained about the advertising dollars that social media personalities could get.

"I'm in the wrong profession," she muttered.

"Right, I –" I stopped and stared at the monitor.

"What?"

I held up a hand. "Hold on." I backed up the video and played it again. "Did you hear that?"

"What?" she repeated.

"I've heard that before," I said.

"You're a Masta Dig fan?"

I rolled my eyes at her. "No. Sally had those same words written down in one of her notebooks." I played the video, called "Get on with It," again. "If I remember right, it's almost word-for-word with what she'd written down."

"What does that mean? Sally helped with the creation of these videos?"

I stared at the screen. "That's what I'm wondering."

"Did she lie to you?"

"It's possible, or Gabe wrote that in her notebook. I haven't been able to ask her what she knows about Masta Dig."

I started listening to other videos, and then something else caught my eye.

"Look at that." I pointed at the monitor again. "The date this video was posted."

She leaned in. "Yesterday."

"Exactly. After Gabe was killed."

"So Masta Dig is acting on his own now."

"But Chase Walker said he thought Gabe was the one who posted the videos, that they were his social media accounts."

"That's not the case, unless this Masta Dig has access to the accounts as well."

"Huh," I said. I handed Humphrey to her and pulled out my phone. "Someone had to create the YouTube, Instagram, Vine, and other accounts. And Masta Dig has his own website. Cal can figure out who's behind all that."

Willie laughed. "Yes, he can."

I called Cal, but he didn't answer. I left a message asking him if he could find the internet account information for Masta Dig, then called Sally again.

"She's still not answering," I said. "She said she doesn't always answer her phone," I said mostly to myself, "but what if something's happened to her?" I pocketed my phone and stood up. "Since Sally isn't returning my calls, I'm going to see if she's home."

"You think someone might've tried to hurt her?"

I shrugged. "I don't know. But I'll worry until I find her."

"Do you want to grab a quick bite? You must be starving."

"I am, but I've got to go."

She frowned. "Be careful, hon, okay? You've been running ragged the last couple of days."

She was clearly worrying, but I needed to talk to Sally.

"I've got to go," I repeated.

She drew in a breath and nodded. "I know. Do what you need to do."

I kissed her, grabbed a light jacket, and headed out the door.

CHAPTER TWENTY-SEVEN

The rain had stopped by the time I reached Sally's apartment, but it was still dark and gloomy, with a chill in the air. I walked down the steps and pounded on the door. A moment later, Sally opened it.

"Hi, Reed," she said, a little startled to see me.

"I've been trying to get hold of you all day," I snapped.

Now that I saw her, and she appeared to be okay, I was furious at her for not answering my calls.

"I, well, I didn't have my phone with me."

"We need to talk." Before she could protest, I pushed past her and looked around.

"Is Kristen here?" I asked.

Sally shook her head. "She's at work. I was doing some writing." She gestured at a notebook and pen on the coffee table.

A lamp in the corner bathed the room in soft light. Music played quietly in the background, but I didn't hear anything else.

"Where is my phone?" she said as she hunted around. She picked up a big purse that was sitting beside the couch and dug into it. Then she held up her cell phone triumphantly. "Ah, here it is. Oh, it's turned off." She pressed the side of it. "Sorry about that."

I threw up my hands. "Are you kidding me? How am I supposed to help you if you won't even answer my calls when I need to talk to you?"

"Uh, well …" She blushed. "I'm sorry." She sat down and stared at me. "What's going on?"

"What do you know about Masta Dig?"

"Who?"

Her face was blank. She had no idea who I was talking about.

"You've never heard of him?"

She shook her head. "No. Who is that? A rapper or something?"

"Where's your laptop?"

"Here." She reached into a backpack, pulled out her laptop, and turned it on. "Why do you need it?"

I sat down next to her. "Search on 'Masta Dig' and go to his Vine channel."

She waited until the laptop had booted up, did as I'd instructed, and found Masta Dig's Vine channel.

"Search for a video called 'Get on with It,'" I said.

She found it and clicked on it. Masta Dig began speaking, and as he continued, Sally's eyes grew wide and her jaw dropped. When it finished, she stared at me.

"I wrote that."

"You did? That's not a lie?"

"*I* did," she said indignantly.

I tapped the notebook on the coffee table. "Is this the notebook I saw the other day? Those lyrics are in there."

"Of course they are. Gabe had the notebook, but I got it back from him." She jabbed a finger at the laptop. "But who the hell is Masta Dig and why is he doing my routine?"

"Gabe said he knew Masta Dig, that they were partners."

"I never heard that."

"It's true, and the partner's still active." I pointed at the laptop. "Look at that one. It was posted yesterday, after Gabe was murdered."

She clicked on the video and played it.

"The concept for this video was something I told Gabe about," she said when it finished. "He said he thought my idea was funny." She scowled. "He stole it from me and let Masta Dig use it." She turned back to the laptop and played more videos. With a few of them, she shook her head angrily.

"Are all the videos your material?" I asked.

"Not all, but there's enough." She gnawed her lip, then repeated, "I've never heard of Masta Dig."

"Gabe had his videos posted on his Facebook page."

"I told you, I don't really do social media, so I never saw it." She swore. "Unbelievable."

"Does Masta Dig look familiar to you?"

She studied another video closely. "His voice seems familiar, but the mask muffles it, and it's like he's talking in a way to disguise it."

"They filmed some of these at an old farmhouse near Roggen," I said. "Did Gabe ever mention going there?"

"I don't think so."

"Masta Dig is really popular. Gabe was trying to get representation for Masta Dig, so they could cash in on advertising dollars."

"Using my material," she said harshly.

"The man Gabe met at Club 77 is Chase Walker. He's an agent."

She shrugged. "Never heard of him." She seemed to be telling the truth. "Did Gabe sign with him?" she asked.

I shook my head. "No, but they were working on a deal."

She called Gabe a few choice words. I couldn't argue. What Gabe had done to her was inexcusable. But I believed her when she'd said she didn't know anything about Masta Dig.

I switched topics. "Why were you going over to your old apartment?"

"When?" She tried to act innocent.

"Yesterday."

"How do you know that? You followed me?"

"This case is about you, Sally, and I need to know if you're hiding something." I stared hard at her. "You said you were going to stay home, or go to your mother's, but that was all."

"I was … seeing someone else. It doesn't matter."

"Who? Was it the man you left Club 77 with the night Gabe met with Chase?"

She started to protest, then stopped. "You know about that?"

"What do you think I've been doing the last few days? I've been asking questions about you and trying to prove your innocence. Not that you seem to care."

"I do!" She took a long time to answer. "I'm embarrassed to say it, but I saw Gabe's friend, Adam."

"You were cheating on Gabe."

"Well …"

"Did you get in a fight about that and you killed him?"

"No!"

She was telling the truth. I thought back to when I'd first visited the Columbine apartment complex and had seen Gabe coming down the stairs. "Is Adam on the second floor?"

She nodded.

"Is he younger, and thin? Kind of scrawny?"

"Uh-huh."

Something fell into place. "Why'd you leave with him that night at Club 77?"

"It was just to piss off Gabe. Nothing came of it."

"But you're seeing Adam now."

"That was just because he wanted my ..." She stopped.

"What?"

"He was asking about my notebooks and the stuff Gabe had scanned onto his computer. Adam told me that Gabe had written some lyrics in my notebooks, and he wanted to see it because it was some music they'd been working on. I didn't believe him, and I didn't give him anything." She sneered. "I said 'Listen, A, you're not getting any of *my* stuff.'"

"Wait." I held up a hand, thinking about what Luis had said to me. "You said what?"

"Huh?"

"You said, 'Listen, eh. Like a Canadian would say?"

She shook her head. "No, I was mocking Adam. Gabe would call Adam by his initial, A. 'Listen, A. What're you doing, A?' Things like that. It was their way of being cool, I guess." She stared at me. "What?"

I told her about my conversation with Luis Hernandez. "He was with Gabe and Masta Dig when they created some of the videos, and he heard Gabe call Masta Dig 'A,' just like you said Gabe would do with Adam."

"Adam is Masta Dig?"

I grimaced. "It sure looks like it."

"I don't understand what's going on."

More things began to make sense. "When I was looking for you, I saw Gabe at the apartment building on Columbine. He was coming down the stairs and he yelled that he should take it all, that he had the material and he could do it himself."

"So?"

I stood up. "If Adam is Masta Dig, he may have killed Gabe."

"Why?"

I thought about what Davon had said about having to split the car-theft money with Gabe. I'd been looking at things wrong. "Gabe thought he could cash in on Masta Dig's popularity and not have to share the money with anyone. He was the one with the connection to Chase Walker, and he had access to your material. I'll bet Gabe and Adam were fighting about that, and when Gabe threatened to go on his own, Adam killed him."

"But a lot of it's my material," she said.

"Exactly. That's why Adam was trying to get your notebooks."

"Oh." She had a few choice words for Adam as well. "I can't believe they were stealing my stuff!"

My phone rang just then. It was Cal.

"O Great Detective," he said. "You did say 'Masta Dig,' right?"

"Yes."

"I did some looking around, and –"

"His website belongs to a man named Adam."

"Yeah, Adam Jance. You figured it out before I did."

"Yeah, but you confirmed it. I've got to go. Thanks for the help."

"No problem. You sound like you're on to something, so be careful."

"Will do." I ended the call and thought for a moment. Something else occurred to me and I turned to Sally. "Did you tell Adam about my investigation?"

"Yes. He was asking about what the police knew, and whether I thought they'd charge me with Gabe's murder."

I was now almost certain it had been Adam who had shot at me in the field behind the farmhouse. He knew I was figuring things out and that I'd be after him soon. But what would he do now? I suddenly was worried for those around me, and I immediately called Ace's cell phone.

"Hey, Reed, how're you?"

"Do you have time for a favor?" I asked.

"Sure."

"Is Deuce there?"

"Yeah. We were about to go play pool."

"Can you put that on hold?"

"How do I hold pool?"

I put a hand to my forehead. "Never mind. Can one of you go upstairs and stay with Willie? And I need one of you to come stay with my client, Sally." I quickly explained what was going on.

"Sure thing, Reed." I heard him tell Deuce what I'd said and to go upstairs. "I'll come over there."

"You remember where she lives?"

"Yep."

"Great. I'll make it up to you."

"No problem. I'm on my way."

I ended the call and turned to Sally. "I might be overreacting, but if I'm right, Adam may come after you because he's worried about what I've told you."

"He would do that?"

"If I'm right, he's killed once, and he shot at me."

She shivered. "I can't believe it."

I went to the window and peeked out.

"When does Kristen get home?" I asked.

"Not until after midnight."

"And you're not expecting anyone else?"

"No."

We didn't say much else until Ace arrived. I let him in and introduced him to Sally.

"Hi," he said. Normally he's shy, but because he was involved in my case, he stood straight, with a stern look on his face.

"Don't go out, and lock the door," I said. "And don't let anyone in except Kristen. Call the police if Adam shows up. I'll touch base with you in a while."

"Gotcha," Ace said with a little salute.

Sally suppressed a smile.

I narrowed my eyes at her. "Answer the phone when I call."

"I will."

I started for the door.

"Where are you going?" she asked.

"I'm going to start at Adam's apartment," I said. "He has a lot of questions to answer."

CHAPTER TWENTY-EIGHT

When I walked into the apartment complex on Columbine, it was quiet. No loud music, no blaring TV coming from any units. I'd put my Glock in my jacket pocket so it would be easy to get to, and I put my hand on it, then tiptoed up the stairs to the second floor. As I neared the second floor landing, I could see down the hall. A man in a hoodie was standing in front of 203, his hand on the doorknob.

"Adam?" I said.

He glanced up, saw me, then bolted the other way.

"Hey!" I yelled and ran up the stairs.

I raced down the hall after him. He turned the corner and was gone. I reached the end of the hall, and saw a stairwell. Adam was already at the bottom of it. As I leaped down the stairs, he opened a door and disappeared. I crashed down the last steps and ran out the door, which led to a parking lot. I looked around and saw a figure heading toward the back of the building. I ran after him. He reached a chain-link fence at the edge of the complex, climbed it, and dropped onto the ground on the other side.

I got to the fence and climbed it, not as adroitly as Adam, so by the time I'd gotten over it, he had vanished around the side of a house. I sprinted through the shadows, and when I came to the front of the house,

I didn't see him anywhere. I hustled over by a tall maple tree and crouched down for a minute and listened. All I heard was my ragged breathing. I scanned the street, but never saw him or anyone else. I finally gave up and sneaked back around the side of the house and over the fence. I went back into the building and up to Adam's apartment. The building was still quiet.

After listening for a moment longer, I tried the knob and the door opened. I let myself into Adam's apartment, quietly shut the door, and turned on a light. I was standing in a small living room that was furnished with a ratty loveseat, a card table with a computer and papers on it, and a TV sitting on a low stand. A poster of Snoop Dogg was on one wall. I'd never been into rap, but I recognized him. Posters of what I assumed were other rappers hung on the other walls. The room smelled of marijuana and bacon, an odd combination.

I immediately went to the computer and moved the mouse. The monitor came to life, but the computer was password-protected. I tried a few things, like Adam's name and Masta Dig, but nothing worked. Next, I checked the papers on the table. Most had handwritten notes on them, and as I read them, I realized they were scripts for Masta Dig videos. I wondered how many of them were from Sally's notebooks. Then I found some paperwork on how to create silicone and latex masks.

For Masta Dig?

I put the papers back and checked the loveseat, where I found my flashlight tucked between the cushions.

Pretty good proof that Adam had been out in that field, I thought. It didn't definitively prove he'd shot at me, but I would still put money on that.

I poked my head into the kitchen and saw nothing out of the

ordinary, so I moved down a short hall, past a tiny bathroom, and into the sole bedroom. A double bed was against one wall, the sheets rumpled. Dirty clothes were tossed on the floor. I checked a dresser in the corner. A bong sat on it, along with a lighter. T-shirts, socks, underwear, and a few other shirts were stuffed into the drawers.

I went to the closet and opened the door. A few pairs of jeans and khaki pants, two long-sleeved shirts, and a leather jacket were on hangers, along with a gray hoodie. I noticed a box on the floor, and I bent down and opened it. Inside was a Masta Dig mask, this one with a weird smiling face. It was creepier than what I'd seen in the videos. Next to the mask were a mannequin head, an empty liquid latex bottle, industrial gypsum, and various paints.

"Everything to create a variety of masks," I muttered.

"What are you doing here?" a severe voice said.

I jumped and stood up, my hand going to the gun in my jacket pocket. The manager was standing in the bedroom doorway.

"Oh, hello," I said as I pulled my hand from my jacket.

He squinted at me through his thick glasses. "Do I know you?"

"No."

Technically that was true. He'd *met* me, but he didn't *know* me.

"Why're you in Adam's apartment?" he asked, his accent thicker than I remembered.

"I'm waiting for Adam. He said if I got here before he did, I should let myself in. I'm just hanging out." The lie slipped out so easily, it almost scared me.

He eyed me suspiciously. "You were here the other day."

"That's true."

He glanced around. "I heard some commotion, and I came to see if there was a problem."

Oh sure, he hadn't managed to hear anything else that went on in the complex, but he'd heard my altercation with Adam and came running?

"You're friends with Adam?" He was still skeptical.

"Yes. I'll tell you what," I said as I stepped by him and headed down the hallway. "I'll wait outside if that'll make you feel more comfortable."

If I didn't get out of there soon, I figured he might call the police, and I didn't need that hassle right now.

He grunted. "I think you should."

We went out into the hall, and he made sure to lock Adam's door. Then he made a show of checking to make sure it was locked. As we turned away from the door, a young woman in tight jeans and a sleeveless blouse came up the stairs.

"Do you know where Adam might be?" I asked the manager.

"I thought you said he was coming back," he said, now even more suspicious.

"Adam's going to a rave," the woman said.

The manager stared at her. "A what?"

"An underground dance party," I said. "Well, some of them are underground."

She eyed me appreciatively. I think she assumed neither of us would know the term.

"Where?" I asked her.

She looked me up and down. "Nowhere you need to be." She laughed as she continued down the hall and let herself into a unit near the other stairwell.

"Huh," I said.

The manager shook his head. "I don't understand young people."

"I'll look for Adam there." I waved my hand at him and started for the stairs.

"What rave?" He was still standing by Adam's door with a confused look on his face.

I rushed outside and back to my car, but I sat for a minute, thinking. How was I going to find a rave party? They were not necessarily advertised, and could be by invite only. I tried the one person I could think of who might know. Sally. This time, she answered.

"What's up?"

"I saw Adam, but he got away," I said.

"Is he coming here?" she asked quickly.

"He's supposed to be at a rave party, but do you know where?"

"Hmm. There's a regular one that's at a warehouse Wednesday nights. Some musicians and rappers go there to try their stuff on a live audience – which is to say, their friends. It's on Thirty-sixth Street, near Wynkoop. Adam sometimes did some performing there. Oh!" She snapped her fingers. "I remember Kristen saying that some masked rapper showed up there a time or two."

"I'll bet that's the one, but I'm assuming there's no sign advertising this place, so do you have an address?"

She laughed. "I don't have any idea. When you get to Wynkoop and Thirty-sixth, go about halfway down the block to an alley. Follow it and there'll be a tan brick building. On the north side, you'll see a black door. Go in there and down the hall, and it's at the end."

"Okay," I said slowly, trying to remember it all. "You doing okay there?"

"Sure. Your friend's a hoot. We've been playing poker."

I smiled. The Goofballs had a way of charming people, and I wasn't surprised she was getting along with Ace.

"Good," I said. "I'll be in touch soon."

I ended the call and headed to Wynkoop Street.

CHAPTER TWENTY-NINE

It was dark when I drove on Thirty-eighth Street and crossed the railroad tracks near Blake. Two blocks down, I turned on Wynkoop and doubled back to Thirty-sixth. I slowed as I drove west. The few streetlights did little to illuminate the area, and I wished the moon would come out from behind some clouds. I was in an older warehouse district, and I couldn't tell if there was a rave going on because the streets were quiet, and I saw few cars around. I drove around the block, but still didn't see any signs of a party.

I came back to Thirty-sixth and saw the alley Sally had mentioned. I parked near it and got out. In the distance, I heard a train, and I heard a dog barking. Then silence. I still had my Glock in my jacket pocket, and I silenced my phone before starting down the alley. My footsteps sounded loud on the pavement. I passed an abandoned warehouse, and next to it I saw the tan brick building Sally had described. It was two stories, with blacked-out windows on the second floor, but no windows on the first. I walked to the north end of the building and listened.

Now I thought I heard the thump of music, but I couldn't be sure.

I stepped past a Dumpster and followed a dirt path along the side of the building, and then found the black door Sally had mentioned. I tried the knob and it turned. I guess the rave wasn't big on security. I opened the door and stepped into a long hallway, and now I did hear music and voices. I walked down the hall and turned left. The music grew louder, a pounding bass beat. At the end of a hall, a few people milled outside of another closed door, smoking and talking. As I walked toward them, they eyed me warily.

"What do you want?" a girl with short black hair and lots of tattoos asked.

I gestured at the door. "I want to party."

"Who told you about us?" This from a man with dreadlocks down to the middle of his back.

"Adam Jance," I said.

Dreadlocks stared at me for a moment longer, then stepped aside. "Go on in."

I opened the door and went inside. Music, cigarette and marijuana smoke, and strobe lights assaulted me. I was in a small room with high ceilings. A few people milled around the edges of the room, and in the center, several bodies gyrated in rhythm to loud techno music. I found myself moving with the beat as I began to look around. I received more than a few stares, and I overheard someone say "cop" to their friend. I needed to find Adam fast, before everyone left because they thought I was part of some kind of police raid.

I made my way around the throng on the dance floor and toward a small, makeshift stage. Two men were standing behind electronic equipment, talking to each other, one wearing a black hoodie. He turned and I saw his face.

Adam.

He had a bottle of beer in one hand, and he was watching the dancers, eyeing one woman in particular. I started toward him and then he looked my way. He recognized me immediately and threw his bottle at me. I ducked as he darted around the other side of the stage and vanished behind the sea of dancers.

I pushed my way through the crowd and more than a few people cursed at me. I made it to the other side of the stage and saw Adam going through an exit. I rushed after him, ran into a woman who was writhing to the music and had to untangle myself from her, and finally made it to the door. I shoved it open and burst into an alleyway, right into a group of smokers who were standing around, drinking from a liquor bottle. The moon had made an appearance, and the alleyway was barely illuminated. Directly across from me was the abandoned warehouse that I'd passed before. I glanced around. Adam was at one end of the alleyway, but had run into a high fence with barbed wire at the top. He spun around, saw me, and scrammed through a door into the abandoned warehouse.

"Hey, watch it," a man said as I pushed through the drinking group.

"Sorry," I muttered and took off after Adam.

I ran to the end of the alleyway, wrenched the door open, then paused by the wall. Adam had shot at me before, and it was possible he'd do it again. I pulled my Glock from my jacket and held it up, then peeked around the corner. I didn't see Adam, so I stepped inside. To the left was an open door and I crouched down and looked through the doorway.

Empty.

On the other side of the hallway was another open door. I glanced into a large room. Moonlight filtered in from broken windows and shone on a few tables, chairs, and cardboard boxes. Then I heard a thump. I peered into the shadows and saw a figure at the other end of the room.

"Adam, stop!" I called out.

He turned around and swore at me. A shot rang out, but it went wild. I ducked down as he disappeared through another door. I ran across the room and almost tripped over a table. When I reached the door, I again cautiously poked my head in the doorway. A stairwell led to the second floor. I aimed the Glock in front of me and hurried up. There was a long, dark hallway and I tiptoed down it, glancing into empty rooms. I reached the end and was about to check another room when I heard something around the corner. I peered around it and saw Adam trying to force open a window. He had a gun in his right hand.

I put my arm around the corner and raised the Glock at him. "Drop the gun and don't move."

Adam spun around and swung his gun toward my voice. I ducked down, aimed at his right arm, and pulled the trigger. Adam jerked to the left and cried out. His gun clattered to the floor as he sank down by the window.

"You shot me!" he hollered.

He put his left hand on his right biceps, groaned, and then swore a blue streak.

I darted into the hall and kicked his gun away before he had a chance to react. Then I stood back and aimed the Glock at him.

"You were going to shoot me," I said.

"Man, it hurts."

"You'll live."

I pulled out my phone and dialed 911, then reported a shooting at the warehouse. The dispatcher tried to keep me on the line, but I ended the call, and dialed Spillman.

"You calling me late can't be a good thing," she said when she answered.

"I've got Gabe Culpepper's killer," I said, then told her where I was.

She didn't mince any words. "I'll be there as fast as I can."

I ended the call and stared at Adam.

"You did kill Gabe, right?" I said to him.

"I'm not talking to you," he growled.

"He was the one with the talent." I egged him on to see if he'd talk. "You were just riding on his coattails, hoping he would lead you to the big bucks. He wrote the scripts, told you what to do, talked to people about representation. You didn't have any talent at all."

My badgering worked, and he lost it.

"That's not true! I'm Masta Dig. *I* got the talent. All Gabe had was Sally's scripts, and he did some producing, but I came up with ideas, too. I'm the one that made everything work."

"You stole a lot of Sally's material."

He clamped his mouth shut.

"You've been hanging around Gabe's apartment, trying to get in. One of the neighbors saw you. And you tried to get Sally to give you her notebooks."

"I did not," he said sullenly.

"I heard Gabe talking to you," I went on, "the first day I was looking for Sally. He said he was going to take all the money."

"I have as much a right to that money, if not more."

"So you killed him."

"That's not what happened."

"What did happen?"

The sound of sirens sounded in the distance.

"I'm not talking to you," he said. He held his arm and grimaced again. "It was an accident," he murmured.

I shrugged. "That's between you and the police."

He glared at me. I leaned against the wall, the Glock still on him. He wasn't going anywhere. He was finished.

"Why'd you have to get greedy?" I said. "There would've been plenty of money to go around."

"Shut up."

"Did you call Chase Walker about representing you?"

"Not yet."

"You wanted to wait until the police gave up on Gabe's murder, and everything cooled down, and then you'd make your move."

He didn't say anything to that.

I tried to get him to talk more, but he stared past me, his mouth a thin, pained line. I finally heard commotion down the hallway and I yelled for the police. Two uniforms appeared and they rushed at me, guns drawn. I explained who I was, and while I was doing that, Detective Spillman showed up and took charge.

After that, a flurry of activity ensued. The officers talked to Adam and arrested him, and I spent a long time talking to Spillman. I called Sally and told her what had happened, and then I called Deuce. I thanked him for his help and told him to go home. Finally, in the wee hours of the morning, I went home as well.

CHAPTER THIRTY

I slept late the next morning. Willie had to work, and I'd briefly told her what had happened before she took a shower and got ready. We'd agreed that I'd take her to dinner that night, and when she left, I fell back asleep. Bogie's voice woke me a few hours later. I picked up my phone and answered.

"Reed, dear? Are you still sleeping?"

"Hello, Mother," I yawned as Humphrey leaped onto my chest and stared at me.

"Just when I think that you're okay, and that you're taking care of yourself, not doing drugs, I find you –"

"I worked almost all night," I interrupted.

"Oh." Her annoyance went away. "I was calling to see about Brenda and Sally."

"It's all over." I sat up in bed and told her what had happened.

"That's wonderful to hear. I'm sure Brenda will be so pleased. Thank you for helping them."

"Glad to do it."

"It's good to see you doing well. Now if you would just give me some grandchildren."

There it was. My mother'd had a few concerns over the years, wondering whether I was doing drugs, and whether I'd get married. Those had been put to rest, but now she wanted her third concern – grandchildren – addressed.

I glanced at Humphrey. "How about a grandkitten first?"

"What?"

I told her about Humphrey.

"Well, that's cute, I guess."

I laughed. "Don't worry, Mother. We'll get around to grandkids someday."

"Fine." She sounded disappointed.

We chatted for a few minutes longer, and then I told her I needed to call Sally. So she hung up, but not before telling me she was proud of me. That was nice to hear. I stretched and went into the kitchen and while I prepared coffee, I checked my phone.

Sally had called and said she'd been at the police station, then asked if I could meet Brenda and her at the Starbucks at noon. I looked at the microwave clock. Almost eleven. I'd have enough time to shower and get there in time. I called her back, but she didn't answer – of course – so I left a message saying I'd be there. Then I stopped making coffee, since I'd be having some soon, and went to take a shower.

» » » » »

When I arrived at the Starbucks, Brenda and Sally were sitting at a table outside. The previous evening's rain had gone, and it was pleasantly warm. Sally hopped up when she saw me.

"Let me get you a drink," she said. "A caramel macchiato?"

"That'll work."

I sat down while she went inside. Brenda looked wan, but there was a sparkle in her eyes. She reached across the table and gave my hand a squeeze.

"Thank you so much."

I nodded. "I'm glad it worked out okay."

"Me, too. I feel better than I have in months."

I smiled.

"Take this." She pushed a check across the table.

I glanced at it. The sum was much more than I deserved.

"You earned it," she said as if reading my mind, "so don't argue."

I thanked her, folded the check, and put it in my pocket. We sat in contemplative silence until Sally returned.

"Here you go." She set a glass down in front of me.

"Thanks." I took a sip. "Hmm, that's good." Then I looked at them. "What did the police say?"

"Quite a lot," Sally said, "but I'll skip the details you already know. They took Adam to the hospital and treated him for a flesh wound in his arm. By the way, did you mean to hit him in the arm?"

"Yes," I said. "I wanted him to drop the gun, which he did."

"Nice shot."

I arched an eyebrow. "I go to the shooting range, too."

She smiled. "Anyway, what's important is that Adam finally caved and told them he'd shot Gabe. He said it was an accident."

"Where'd he get the gun?"

"From a cousin who stole it a while back." Sally gestured at me. "You figured it correctly. Adam and Gabe had created all the Masta Dig videos together, but Gabe thought he deserved more of the money, since he was the one coming up with most of the ideas, a lot of which were actually mine." She waved a hand dismissively. "Anyway, Adam said they'd argued about that the night I went over to Gabe's apartment, and he'd threatened Gabe with the gun and it went off accidentally."

"That sounds like an excuse," Brenda interjected.

I nodded.

Sally went on. "Adam heard me at the door, so he took off down the fire escape. He thought he'd get away with it, and he figured he could assume the role of Masta Dig on his own. Then he realized you were poking around, and so he came after you."

"Was he watching my place the other night?"

Sally nodded. "That was after I talked to him. Sorry, I didn't know what was going on."

"Huh," I said. "He must've Googled me and found my address."

I didn't like it when *others* used the Internet to find *me*.

"I'm just glad he didn't harm you or your wife," Brenda said.

I laughed wryly. "Me, too." I looked at Sally. "Will you get your notebooks back?"

"Yes, and I plan to see what I can do with everything I've written. Maybe there's a future for *me* as a social media personality."

Brenda repressed a sigh.

"But don't worry," Sally said quickly, "I'm still keeping my day job, and I'm going to save up for my own place."

"Sounds like a good plan," I said.

Brenda smiled, and Sally nodded. We'd said what needed to be said, and I could tell the two of them wanted time to themselves. I thanked them, took my drink, and left. On the way to my car, my phone rang. Spillman.

"You get some sleep?" she asked without preamble.

"Some," I said. "You?"

"Not yet. Did you talk to Sally?"

"Just now. You got your man."

"Thanks to you. But I wish you'd shared what was going on."

"I didn't have any proof."

She sighed. "One of these days, you're going to get into a real jam."

"One of these days?"

She laughed. "Oh, before I forget, I passed along the information about Davon Edwards, and some detectives went to question him. He's being very careful right now, but we've got our eye on him. If he steals another car, we'll get him."

"I hope so."

"You take care of yourself."

"You, too," I said, but she'd already hung up.

》 》 》 》 》

I spent the rest of the day doing my own thank-yous. I drove up to Cal's house and since he didn't like to go out, I brought a nice take-out lunch to him. And when I got home, the Goofballs had just returned from work, so I took them to play pool. After several games, I left them at B 52's and headed home. When I walked in the door, Willie was wearing a black skirt and a sleeveless blouse, ready for dinner.

"You look great," I said.

"You told me to dress nice." She brushed at the skirt. "It's a good thing Humphrey has black fur, so you can't see it on this." Humphrey tried to crawl up her legs and she distracted him with a toy. "He's cute, but he has so much energy."

I laughed at her predicament. "But he is a nice addition to our home."

She smiled. "I'm glad you feel that way.

I nodded. "Give me a minute to change and we'll go."

"Where are you taking me?"

"Elway's," I said.

"Oh, fancy."

I kissed her, then hurried to the bedroom. As I got ready, I thought about Sally again. She might be a nightmare, a tame version of Tyrone Power in *Nightmare Alley*, but whereas his life was ruined, she seemed to be moving ahead. I hoped she would achieve her dreams, just as I had.

AUTHOR'S NOTE

Detective Sarah Spillman appears in three short stories: *Seven for Suicide*, *Saturday Night Special*, and *Dance of the Macabre*. Each are published individually in ebook format, and are also included in the short story collection, *Take Five*. *Take Five* also includes a Reed Ferguson short story, *Elvis And The Sports Card Cheat*.

ABOUT THE AUTHOR

Renée Pawlish is the author of The Reed Ferguson mystery series, the Dewey Webb historical mystery series, *Nephilim Genesis of Evil*, The Noah Winter adventure series, *This War We're In* (middle-grade historical novel), *Take Five*, a short story collection that includes a Reed Ferguson mystery, and The *Sallie House: Exposing the Beast Within*, about a haunted house investigation in Kansas.

Renée loves to travel and has visited numerous countries around the world. She has also spent many summer days at her parents' cabin in the hills outside of Boulder, Colorado, which was the inspiration for the setting of Taylor Crossing in her novel *Nephilim*.

Visit Renée at www.reneepawlish.com.

The Reed Ferguson Mystery Series
This Doesn't Happen In The Movies
Reel Estate Rip-off
The Maltese Felon
Farewell, My Deuce
Out of the Past
Torch Scene
The Lady Who Sang High
Sweet Smell of Sucrets
The Third Fan
Back Story
Night of the Hunted
The Postman Always Brings Dice
Road Blocked
Small Town Focus
Nightmare Sally
Ace in the Hole (novella)
Walk Softly, Danger (Kindle Worlds novella)
Elvis And The Sports Card Cheat (short story)

A Gun For Hire (short story)

The Dewey Webb Mystery Series
Web of Deceit
Murder In Fashion
Secrets and Lies
Honor Among Thieves
Second Chance (short story)

The Nephilim Trilogy
Nephilim Genesis of Evil
Books Two and Three soon to be released

The Noah Winter Adventure Series
The Emerald Quest
Dive into Danger
Terror on Lake Huron
Book Four coming soon

This War We're In
Middle-grade historical fiction

Take Five
A Short Story Collection

The Sallie House: Exposing the Beast Within
Non-fiction account of a haunted house investigation in Kansas

Made in the USA
Lexington, KY
17 May 2019